Many Happy Returns, Mrs. Entwhistle

Doris Reidy

Additional Titles by Doris Reidy

Doris Reidy

Dedication

For my family, who feel like dear friends

and my dear friends, who feel like family.

CONTENTS

Mrs. Entwhistle and the Disciples of Holiness

CHAPTER ONE

Mrs. Entwhistle had a time convincing Roger to get into the car for his trip to the vet's. Somehow the old dog knew where they were headed, and he resisted with all his might. Roger would never bite—he hardly ever even growled, except at chipmunks—but he planted all four feet on the ground and increased his twelve-pound body weight by a factor of ten. Mrs. Entwhistle was impressed by his ability to make himself so heavy, but, as always, her leverage and opposable thumbs won out. He was bundled into the car, where he began crying piteously.

"For heaven's sake, Roger. It's just for a quick blood test. Okay, you'll have to sit on the exam table, and there will be a needle stick, but you'll hardly feel it."

Roger was not comforted by this description of his near future and continued to weep softly. Mrs. Entwhistle felt like a monster, but she persevered. She'd had to borrow her daughter, Diane's, car for the vet visit since Roger couldn't ride with her on her scooter, and she was determined to get her mission accomplished. The older Roger got, the harder it was to take him anyplace.

Predictably, his nerves got the better of him in the parking lot, and Mrs. Entwhistle had to get a plastic bag from the outdoor dispenser and clean up after him. He protested all the way in the clinic door, finally decided further resistance was futile and lay trembling on her lap.

"We're here for Dr. Goodlet," Mrs. Entwhistle called from where she sat. "I'm bringing Roger Entwhistle for his six-month blood work."

The girl behind the desk nodded, smiled and dived head-first into her computer screen. Mrs. Entwhistle waited. Half an hour passed, and Roger finally stopped shaking, too worn out from anxiety to sustain the effort.

"Is it going to be much longer?" Mrs. Entwhistle called again. "Because our appointment was for ten, and it's ten-thirty."

"I'm sorry, Mrs. Entwhistle, but Dr. Goodlet hasn't come in yet."

"Hasn't come in? Where is he?"

"We haven't heard from him. Would you like to see one of the vet techs?"

"Well, all right, I guess. It's just a blood draw. I expect a tech could do it just fine."

This was duly accomplished and Roger relaxed in the front seat of the car, limp with relief that his ordeal was over. Mrs. Entwhistle wondered all the way home what had happened to make always-dependable Dr. Goodlet absent without so much as a word to his staff.

~*~

Mrs. Entwhistle dropped Roger off for a nap on his favorite sofa cushion, then took Diane's car to the school where she worked. She left it in the parking lot in Diane's usual space. It was a mile's walk home, and Diane would have a fit about the dangers of her getting run down by a car or suffering a heart attack from fatigue, but Mrs. Entwhistle enjoyed walking. As she passed the Busy Bee Diner, she saw the flashing neon sign that said, "Hot Fresh Donuts."

That sign was only lit when the donuts came out of the fryer, which wasn't often enough, to her way of thinking. Mrs. Entwhistle wasn't going to pass up such an opportunity. She entered the diner and took a seat at the counter.

"Two glazed, please, Harvey, and a cup of Earl Grey," she said to the cook, Herve', who was used to people butchering his name. He trotted back and forth between the kitchen and the dining room looking harried and out of sorts.

"Where's Carol Anne?" Mrs. Entwhistle asked.

"She no come in today," Herve' said.

"Is she sick?"

"Don' know. She don' call or nothing."

"Hmmm. Must be something going around."

First Dr. Goodlet, and now Carol Anne. Mrs. Entwhistle hoped it wasn't anything contagious.

Mrs. Entwhistle noticed a little crowd around one of the booths in the back. People were leaning in, craning their necks to see and hear a man who was holding forth. Usually she knew everyone, but she didn't recognize the speaker. She ate both her donuts, forgetting her earlier resolve to take one home for tomorrow. It wouldn't have been as yummy the next day, anyway.

~*~

When she arrived at her house, Mrs. Entwhistle saw Dex and Lara sitting on the front porch swing, holding hands. Her heart lifted, as it always did when she saw them. Dex was one of her dearest friends, despite the age difference between twenty-two and seventy-nine. Lara was his bride, whom Mrs. Entwhistle would have loved for no other reason than because Dex did, but, fortunately, Lara had her own lovable qualities.

"Well, hi, you two," she said. "What a nice surprise."

"We were out running errands and thought we'd stop by," Lara said. "We went to show Rev. McGill our wedding pictures and leave him one for his wall of weddings, but he wasn't there."

"There seems to be a lot of that going around this morning," Mrs. Entwhistle said. "When will he be back?"

"And that's what's so strange," Dex said. "His housekeeper didn't know where he was or when he'd be back. When she got to work this morning, he was gone. She checked at his house and found that his bed hadn't been slept in, the coffee pot was cold, and there was no note. I suppose he got called away to some parishioner's bedside or something."

"Oh, I'm sure you're right. Rev. McGill probably had to hurry to someone who needed him," Mrs. Entwhistle said. "It's funny Rita didn't know where he was, though. She's usually like LoJack where he's concerned. Well, never mind. He'll turn up. Let's have a look at those pictures."

Mrs. Entwhistle picked up the phone to call her best friend, Maxine. It had been a couple of days since she and Max had talked, which was unusual. Ordinarily they talked every day. The phone went to voice mail, but Mrs. Entwhistle didn't leave a message. She knew Max would check her missed calls and get in touch.

She settled down with her book of crossword puzzles, but couldn't concentrate. A feeling of unease made her gaze at the window and listen for Maxine's car in the drive. A dozen times she checked to make sure her cell phone was turned on. Finally, she rose and took her motorcycle helmet off the hook by the door. Roger looked up blearily from his nest of sofa cushions.

"I'm just going over to Maxine's," she told him. "You go back to sleep. I won't be long."

But when she got to Maxine's house, the door was locked, and there was no response to her repeated knocks and calls. Peeking in the garage, she saw that Maxine's new red car was there. She rapped on the back door and heard angry yowling in response. That would be Martin, Maxine's big orange tomcat. He didn't sound happy. Mrs. Entwhistle felt a tingling in her spine that signaled trouble.

Of course, she and Maxine had keys to each other's houses; Mrs. Entwhistle took out her key-ring and opened the door. Martin launched himself at her, winding around her legs and mewing at full volume. Mrs. Entwhistle saw his food and water bowls were empty, and she smelled that his litter box was full.

"For heaven's sake, Marty," she said, going to the pantry for the bag of cat food. "Where's your mama? Maxine? Maxine? Are you home? Are you all right?"

No answer, just the thick quiet of an empty house, broken only by Martin's emphatic munching.

"Well, I swan," Mrs. Entwhistle said aloud. "Where is everybody today?"

~*~

Mrs. Entwhistle didn't know what else to do but bundle Martin into his cat carrier and take him home with her. She knew it would not be a popular move with Roger, but the poor cat couldn't be left to languish in an empty house. Reflecting on Martin's beginnings as an orphaned kitten who'd had to board at a vet's office, share an adopted mother and survive a car wreck, she figured he'd already run through several of his nine lives. Not a cat fancier herself, she'd care for Martin because Maxine loved him. It wasn't easy securing the carrier onto her scooter, but she managed, riding home to a soundtrack of feline displeasure.

Her head echoed with the question: Where was Maxine?

She considered calling Maxine's daughter, Geraldine, who lived in Australia. But what would that accomplish except to get Geraldine all riled up? She certainly couldn't do anything but worry at such a distance. No, Mrs. Entwhistle would have to figure it out on her own. Well, not completely on her own. She was not without resources. When she got home, she'd call Pete Peters, Deputy U.S. Marshall.

She and Pete went 'way back. He'd taken a bullet trying to protect her after she'd been mistakenly swept into the witness protection program. She'd returned the favor by giving him CPR and saving his life. Now his baby daughter was named Cora, and Pete was her devoted friend.

But before she could call him, the animals had to be settled. When she deposited the cat carrier on her kitchen floor, Martin emerged with his tail lashing and a murderous look in his eye. Roger, who'd come to see what was going on, backed away precipitously. He remembered the swipe Martin had given his nose at their first meeting. Roger had great respect for cats, including the monster next door that tormented him on a regular basis.

"Here you go, Martin," Mrs. Entwhistle said, depositing food and water dishes on the floor. "Now what will I do about a litter box?"

Martin gave her a glance that clearly conveyed it was not his problem. He sniffed and rejected his food, then strolled into the living room and curled up on Roger's favorite sofa cushion. Roger turned sad eyes to Mrs. Entwhistle, who shook her head in sympathy.

"Well, he's company, Rog. We just have to put up with him."

She improvised a cardboard box with some shredded newspaper for Martin's bathroom needs, resolving to pick up cat litter as soon as possible, then picked up her phone and dialed Pete Peters' number. As she'd expected, she had to leave a message.

"Pete, it's Mrs. Entwhistle. I need to ask you about some peculiar things that are going on around here. I can't find Maxine, that's the most worrying one, and other people aren't where they should be, either. Call me back, please."

Pete returned her call within fifteen minutes. "Hey, what's up?"

"Have you heard about anything odd or different that's going on around town?"

"I've been away, just got home last night, so I'm a bit out of touch. Sheila did mention something about a new preacher from a start-up church, the Disciples of something or other, she said. He'd knocked on our door and invited her to attend a service."

"Does she plan to go?"

"No, she said there was something about him that kind of freaked her out."

"Huh. Well, Max never mentioned meeting anybody like that. Where could she have gotten to, Pete? It's not like her to go off without telling me, and she left Martin home alone."

Pete could shed no more light on Maxine's disappearance, but promised to ask around and let Mrs. Entwhistle know if he heard anything. "Don't worry too much," he advised. "I'm sure she'll turn up with a perfectly logical explanation."

Mrs. Entwhistle couldn't help worrying, though. Maxine had a headful of common sense, but was apt to let her soft heart lead her into all sorts of difficulties. Peeking into the living room she saw that Martin and Roger were both sleeping peacefully, although Roger had to settle for the recliner. Tiptoeing to avoid the reproachful eyes she knew would follow her if they saw her leaving, she got her helmet and let herself quietly out the back door. She headed to the Shady Rest Assisted Living Center. It had occurred to her to ask the residents what they'd been hearing. That place was like a native drum, beating out gossip signals from all points of the compass.

When she got there, she found Jacinta in the common room working on her counted cross stitch. Mrs. Entwhistle paused to admire her tiny stitches. Jacinta wasn't too smart, but she still had good eyes, you had to give her that.

"Good morning, Jacinta," she said, raising her voice to accommodate Jacinta's hearing loss. Mrs. Entwhistle knew better than to inquire after her health. That would get you a good hour of symptom discussion and an intimate tour of Jacinta's pill-box. "What's the latest news?" she asked instead.

"Why, Cora, good morning. It's not your regular day. Where's Maxine?"

"I don't know. I seem to have lost track of her, and I was wondering if any of y'all had heard of any special events or, I don't know, church trips, or whatever, that she might have forgotten to mention to me."

"You can't find her? Why, you and Maxine are practically joined at the hip. Something must be wrong if *you* don't know where she is. Say, do you think it's the Rapture?" Jacinta's eyes grew huge. "There was a preacher that came around and talked about what all will happen when the Rapture comes. 'The pure in heart will be taken up to heaven in a cloud,' he said, 'and the ones left behind won't know what happened to them.'"

"No, I'm sure it's not the Rapture," Mrs. Entwhistle said firmly. "Although Maxine would get taken up if anybody would. Who's this preacher I keep hearing about?"

"He said his name was Emanuel. He's starting a new church, the Disciples of Holiness, and he invited everyone to come visit his mission at the old Jenkins place. See, he left these pamphlets." Jacinta pointed to a neat stack on a nearby table.

"Did anyone from here go?"

"Just Clem and Jane Dearing. Clem still drives, you know, and they're always looking for something to do that gets them out of here. I really don't know why they left their home and moved in. Jane *is* a little confused, but Clem's still sharp. Seems like they could have managed at home for a while longer."

"What was their take on this preacher?"

"Why, I don't think I've talked to them since. Can't think when I saw them last." Jacinta bowed her head over her work, her lips moving as she counted stitches. "Oh, dear, now I've lost count."

"I'll leave you to it, then," Mrs. Entwhistle said. She went to find Clem Dearing.

She walked down the long, straight hallway, looking at the names on the doors on either side. When she came to the Dearings, she rapped on the door. Then rapped again. Then called their names. There was no response. She made her way to the lobby and asked the receptionist to call them. The phone rang six times before it went to their voice mailbox, which was full.

"Do you know where they've gone?" Mrs. Entwhistle asked.

"Why, no, they didn't let anyone know they were going away," the receptionist said. "I'll inform the director."

"You do that," Mrs. Entwhistle said.

For heaven's sake. What good did it do to live in assisted living if no one even knew when you weren't there?

CHAPTER TWO

"I don't want to say Maxine is a missing person," Mrs. Entwhistle said carefully, "but I don't know where she is. Her car is at home, but she's not, and she left her cat alone for at least a day and a night, maybe longer. I'm pretty sure everything's fine and there's just been some kind of misunderstanding. I don't want to embarrass her when she turns up by making a big fuss. But still, I am a little worried."

"Yes, ma'am, I understand," Sheriff Trevino said. "I'll tell my deputies to have a quiet look around and see what we can dig up." He caught himself. "I mean, find out."

Mrs. Entwhistle suppressed a shudder at his choice of words, but she let it pass. No sense in blowing things out of proportion. *When you hear hoof beats, think horse, not zebra*, she reminded herself. Occam's Razor: the obvious explanation is usually the right one. But what was the obvious explanation for Maxine's disappearance? It was completely out of character, and Mrs. Entwhistle couldn't help imaging the worst.

There was only one thing to do: make cookies. Chocolate chip cookies helped just about any situation, and besides, they made the house smell heavenly while they were baking. She'd take some to Maxine when she came home.

She tried calling again, but there was no answer. Where the heck was Max? Even that time she'd gone to Australia to see Geraldine, she'd e-mailed or texted every day. The cookie she was sampling turned to sawdust in her mouth. Martin padded into the kitchen, sat down with his tail curled around his body and stared at her through slitted eyes. She immediately felt guilty, as though she were somehow responsible for Maxine's absence.

"I know, Martin, I know. I wish she'd come home, too. If you could only talk, maybe you could tell me where she's gone."

Martin lowered himself onto his belly, stretched luxuriously and dropped suddenly into sleep. Well, everyone knew cats didn't pine.

~*~

Maxine's head was splitting. She raised a trembling hand to her forehead and pressed hard on her temple. What was wrong with her? Her memory of the recent past wavered like a heat mirage on pavement. She'd been at home...cleaning her pantry...someone knocked on the door, and.... Nothing after that. Raising her head, she saw she was lying on a cot in a dim room. Gradually, the stirrings and throat-clearings of others told her she was not alone. But where was she?

She couldn't keep her eyes open no matter how hard she tried. With a start, she realized she'd been dozing again. Her shadowy roommates stirred and mumbled in their cots. Was this a hospital? Had she been ill? Her mouth was so dry her lips stuck to her teeth. She saw a pitcher of water and a glass on a nearby table and managed to pour herself a drink which she downed in three gulps. Instead of reviving her, the water seemed to make her even sleepier. She struggled against the encroaching tidal wave of sleep. But not for long.

~*~

Gus woke in the same room as Maxine. He, too, clutched his pounding head and reached for the water pitcher.

17

Around him, others were waking and looking about dazedly. An aggressively-cheerful man and woman appeared and rousted everyone out of bed. The females were shepherded off in one direction, while the man led the male contingent in another. Later, showered, shaved, combed, dressed, and wider awake, the group met again in a dining room. The meal they were served consisted of steel-cut oatmeal, yogurt and orange juice. Repeated pleas for coffee were ignored by the smiling servers, who refilled water glasses instead.

Gus felt a kind of brain fog he'd never experienced before, not even in veterinary school when he'd studied all night and gone directly to his part-time job as a vet tech. Then, exhaustion and malnutrition had only seemed to sharpen his brain.

"But I was younger then," he said aloud.

"Weren't we all?" his neighbor agreed. "I can't figure out why I'm here. Or where I am, for that matter. Do you know?"

"No. I'm wondering the same thing."

Gus finished his glass of water, dimly aware that his brain was becoming even foggier. It was alarming, but then it didn't seem to matter. He relaxed, meeting the smiles that traveled around the room.

People were quiet, peacefully waiting for whatever happened next.

Gus allowed his mind to drift. It floated gently down memory lane, touching here and there like thistledown. He was back in his first-grade classroom, standing close to his teacher, Mrs. Gentry, on whom he had a giant, six-year-old crush. He could see her kind eyes, feel her cool hand on his head.

"Why, Gus, I believe you have a touch of fever," she said. "Do you feel sick?"

And just at that moment, his stomach confirmed that he was indeed sick by emptying itself on the floor. Tears of embarrassment filled his eyes, but Mrs. Gentry was a pro. It took more than a little upchuck on her shoe to faze her.

"Don't worry about it, Gus," she said, "we have special magic dust to clean it up."

Gus wished for magic dust to clean up his mind right now, but when none appeared, he drifted again. Now he was explaining to Tiffany that he couldn't go to Florida on spring break because he had to study for his MCAT, Medical College Admission Test, as he prepared to apply to veterinarian school.

"But everyone else is going," Tiffany said. He'd never noticed before how she stuck out her lower lip when she was mad.

"You go ahead with the others," he said, "but if I don't study, I won't be admitted. My whole future depends on it."

"Oh it's always all about you," Tiffany said scornfully. "As if a few days in the sun would make any difference. You're no fun."

Sadly, he reflected that she'd gotten that right. She'd found a boy who was more fun and gone to Florida while he'd studied. That was the last he saw of Tiffany.

His hard work had paid off. He was a vet with his own practice, although he had to admit the reality fell short of the dream. He'd graduated with a crushing amount of school debt and spent every day working flat out. Gus was exhausted just thinking about it. Much as he loved his work, it had been a stressful past few years. No wonder he couldn't concentrate.

Vaguely, he wondered who was covering his office. He must have gotten someone in, a *locum tenens* perhaps. But why? What was he doing here? He should be seeing patients right now. It was important. He needed to get back to his office. He started to rise, but a hand on his shoulder eased him back down into his seat. Another hand refreshed his water glass. He drank deeply. So thirsty; his mouth felt like cotton. In a few minutes, the urgency faded from his mind.

~*~

Carol Anne never missed work. It was her lifeline, going to her shift at the Busy Bee Diner every day, interacting with her customers. She starched and ironed her white aprons until they could have stood alone, tied a colorful ribbon around her pony tail and tucked a lace hankie into her pocket. Life hadn't turned out as she'd expected, but she made the best of it.

Carol Anne had a college degree she never got to use. She had a devoted group of customers whom she thought of as friends. They came in especially to see her, and she made it her mission to serve their hearts and minds as well as their stomachs. Discussions ranged from the day's headlines to what, exactly, Camus was driving at in *The Plague*. Those conversations were her gift to herself. It didn't hurt with tips, either.

She worked breakfast and lunch shifts, Tuesday through Saturday, and she was always there on time and ready to work. Now she wondered who was waiting on her tables. Why wasn't she? It was hard to think, and she couldn't focus long enough to figure it out. Her head felt light and insecurely attached to her neck. She put up her hands to hold it on, in case it floated up to the ceiling. As she did, she saw a familiar face.

"Maxine?" Carol Anne said. "What are you doing here? Do you know where we are? Or why we came?"

The white-haired lady across from her at the table smiled vacantly, but didn't respond.

"Maxine, its Carol Anne, from the Busy Bee." She knew it could be disorienting to see someone outside their natural habitat, but Maxine continued to look at her blankly.

Carol Anne looked around her. She saw Dr. Goodlet, the new young vet, Rev. McGill from church, and the Dearings, who lived at Shady Rest but came in for breakfast a couple of times a week. She fluttered her fingers and smiled at each of them, but no one responded. Carol Anne knew almost everyone in town, and she thought they knew her, but there seemed to be some kind of short-circuit today. She looked at her plate and picked at her food, but she couldn't eat because of the lump in her throat.

Apparently, I'm just an anonymous hand setting food

in front of them. They're not my friends at all, not like I thought they were.

She nodded at the server offering more water.

~*~

Mrs. Entwhistle grew more and more concerned about Maxine's whereabouts. Never in their life-long friendship had she disappeared without a word. She went back to Maxine's house and this time she ventured into the basement, timidly calling "Maxine? Maxine?" dreading what she might find. The basement was swept clean and empty of humanity. Then she went up into the attic, although what she expected to find there, she wasn't sure. Plastic storage bins were what she did find, neatly labeled and stacked. She looked into the garage, into the back seat of Maxine's car and even into the little garden shed at the bottom of the yard. When she was totally sure Maxine was in none of those places, she called the sheriff again.

"I still can't find Maxine, and it's been a couple days. I think we'd better start searching," she said.

"Oh, no, ma'am, that won't be necessary. I thought you'd have heard. Maxine is staying at the old Jenkins farm."

"What? Why? What would she be doing out there?"

"Apparently, she's joined that new church, the Disciples of Holiness. She was with some other church members handing out tracts in the town square yesterday."

Yesterday? Mrs. Entwhistle was surprised no one had mentioned seeing Maxine in such company. Ronnie Sue's hair salon was right on the square; you'd think she'd have noticed and told Mrs. Entwhistle. The important thing, though, was that Maxine had been seen alive and well. Mrs. Entwhistle admitted to herself for the first time that she'd feared her friend had met with a terrible misadventure. She felt such a rush of relief that her knees went wobbly. She sat down abruptly.

"I hadn't heard. Did she look all right? Did anyone talk to her?"

"I don't know. I didn't see her myself, but my deputy told me about it. He said the church folks were all wearing some kind of white robes and they were smiling, so I guess she must have looked okay to him. Point is, Maxine isn't missing. She's an adult and free to come and go as she pleases."

As soon as she hung up, Mrs. Entwhistle hopped on her scooter and went to the editorial offices of the town newspaper, the *Pantograph*. As the local beat reporter, the oldest in captivity as she always said, she smelled a story. She'd have a word with her editor, Jimmy Jack McNamara, and hope for an assignment to investigate the Disciples of Holiness. It would serve a double purpose because she'd be able to make sure Maxine was really all right.

She found him in his glass-walled office, peering at his computer screen. That's all anyone seems to do nowadays, she thought, not hesitating to interrupt him.

"Mr. McNamara, I want a few minutes of your time, please."

"Oh, hello, Mrs. Entwhistle," Jimmy Jack said, reluctantly raising his head.

"What do you know about this new church, the Disciples of Holiness?"

"Not much. The preacher is a guy who calls himself Emanuel. No last name. He just kind of turned up, and nobody seems to know anything about him. I hear he's renting the old Jenkins farm and has some folks living with him out there. Bunch of them came to the square yesterday and passed out some kind of literature, I'm told. Surprising, who all was in that group. That new young vet and Carol Anne from the diner, people you wouldn't expect."

"And Maxine," Mrs. Entwhistle said.

"Maxine? Surely not!"

"Apparently so. I haven't been able to find her and just learned today that she's staying at the Jenkins' place. It's not like her to just up and go off without telling me. I don't know what would possess her to do such a thing."

Jimmy Jack shrugged. "I guess she can do what she wants," he began, but Mrs. Entwhistle cut him off.

"Of course she can, nobody disputes that. What I'm saying is, Maxine wouldn't voluntarily up and leave her house and cat and just go. Something isn't right. I'm going to find out what it is."

"Now, Mrs. Entwhistle, the newspaper has no call to go snooping around a church."

Jimmy Jack's face took on familiar lines of worry. Mrs. Entwhistle knew the local beat had beaten him up regularly since he hired her to report on it. There was the money laundering scheme she'd exposed, the Booster Club embezzlement, the kidnapping of one of the town's more famous citizens. Oh, the place had been in an uproar, and even though it had come out all right in the end, Jimmy Jack was still gun-shy. It was all too easy for him to revert to timidity.

Mrs. Entwhistle transfixed him with a Mom-Glare. "If

you don't want me to investigate as a *Pantograph* reporter, I'll do it as a private citizen. But you can bet your boots I won't rest until I know Maxine is well, safe and where she wants to be."

CHAPTER THREE

Rev. Terrence McGill was a rock of dependability. That's what everyone, including his housekeeper, assistant and right-hand gal, Rita, said about him. So it was perhaps more disconcerting that he'd disappeared than it might have been for an ordinary mortal. Rita called everyone she could think of who might have knowledge of his whereabouts. She did her best to reassure parishioners who wanted to talk to him that he'd be back in touch soon. As much as possible, she avoided answering direct questions, copying a skill she saw politicians use every day: don't answer the question, just stay on your talking point.

Her talking point was, "Rev. McGill will be so sorry he missed you. He'll call you back just as soon as he can. Meanwhile, is there anything I can do to be of help?"

It seemed to satisfy most people, but it didn't satisfy Rita. Terry—that's what she called him in her heart—was missing, and she didn't know why. Worse yet, there was no one she could ask. She was grateful when Mrs. Entwhistle seated herself across from her desk and leaned forward confidentially.

"Rita, you can be honest with me. Do you think Rev. McGill might possibly be visiting that new mission? Maxine was spotted with the Disciples of Holiness yesterday, and I'm worried out of my mind about her. It's not like either of them to just go off, and it happened at the same time. That seems suspicious to me."

Rita had been holding her shoulders in a tight knot just below her ears. Now she let them slump at the relief of having someone to share her worry.

"I've been debating if I should file a missing persons report," Rita said. "I don't want to make a big whoop-de-do, and then he comes home with a perfectly logical explanation. He'd be so embarrassed."

"Exactly. I think we should gather more information before we do anything. I'm going to go out there and talk to Max. While I'm at it, I'll see if I can spot Rev.

McGill, too," Mrs. Entwhistle said. "I just need to know if she's there because she wants to be. If she is, I'll leave her alone. But I do need for her to tell me what to do about Martin. Roger isn't happy having him as a houseguest."

"Martin?"

"That's Maxine's cat. She brought him back with her from our trip on Route 66. He's not very nice to my dog, and poor Roger is too old to be tormented by a mean cat in his own house."

"Should I come with you?" Rita asked, but before Mrs. Entwhistle could answer, two lights on the desk phone lit up with incoming calls.

"I think you're needed right here," Mrs. Entwhistle said. "You're the only one holding this place together."

~*~

Mrs. Entwhistle went back to Maxine's place and checked the ignition in Maxine's new car. As she'd suspected, the keys were hanging there invitingly. She sighed and shook her head, parked her scooter and took possession of the car. Maxine wouldn't object if she borrowed it and, after all, she wouldn't have needed to if Maxine had stayed where she belonged.

The Jenkins place was buzzing with activity. Uninhabited for years, it had taken on the forlorn look of vacancy. A shutter hung crazily from one hinge, weeds took over flower beds, shrubs graduated to trees, fields lay fallow. But now there were people working in the sunshine. Sounds of nail guns and power tools filled the air. Mrs. Entwhistle paused at the end of the driveway to take it all in, and that's when she saw Maxine wielding a hedge clipper as she tamed a boxwood at the side of the house.

Mrs. Entwhistle got out of the car and approached her. "Max, how are you?"

Maxine turned. Her eyes and voice were flat. "Oh, hi, Cora. Fine."

"What are you doing here?"

"Trimming this bush." Maxine had become a woman of few words.

"But why?"

"Emanuel said I should."

"Do you feel all right?"

"Fine."

Maxine kept clipping. She was like a robot with her

jerky movements and blank eyes. Mrs. Entwhistle put a hand on Maxine's arm, stilling her movements.

"Let me take you home, Max. Martin misses you. You left him home alone, and he ran out of food and water. He needs you to take care of him. I've got your nice, new car right here. Don't you want to drive it again?"

Maxine's eyes flickered. "Martin? Is he okay?"

Before Mrs. Entwhistle could reply, a heavy hand fell on her shoulder. She turned to face the man she'd seen in the booth at the Busy Bee Diner.

"What's the trouble here?"

"There's no trouble. I'm Cora Entwhistle. I'm here to see my friend, Maxine, and to take her home."

"I am Emanuel." The man had a deep, hypnotic voice that he obviously knew how to use to advantage. "Maxine, please keep on with your trimming, dear. Your friend and I are going to have a little chat."

Maxine nodded, turning back to her work. Emanuel took Mrs. Entwhistle's arm and propelled her toward the house. She shook him off and stopped short.

"I won't go inside," she said firmly. "We can chat here. What's going on? What are you doing, and why are these people with you?"

"They are the Disciples of Holiness, and I am their leader, Emanuel. We are the hope of the world. Where two or three are gathered together...."

She cut him off. "Yes, I'm familiar with the Scripture. But why are you *here* at the Jenkins place, and why are all these folks with you? They have people who are worried about them."

Emanuel looked at her searchingly. "They have come to me willingly, but I can see you don't believe that. Your heart is hard with the arrogance of one who thinks she has all the answers. There is no use talking to you until you are willing to humble yourself. I pray that you be shown the light. You will always be welcome here, my daughter, when you are ready."

That'll be when pigs fly, Mrs. Entwhistle thought, but her instincts were kicking in big-time. Somehow she knew not to go to war with this man, not right now. She gave him a smile so insincere it hurt her face. "I'll just take Maxine back home now, and we can come back later for, um, services."

"Why don't you ask her if she wants to go home?" Emanuel said.

"Good idea. I will." Mrs. Entwhistle went back to

Maxine. "Don't you want to go home, Max? Come on, let's go."

Her naturally loud voice conveyed all the authority of a decades-long friendship. Maxine's head slowly turned; her eyes brightened a bit. Dropping her clippers, she took a step, but Emanuel was suddenly at her side.

"Come now, dear, you haven't finished your job. A good disciple never leaves a job uncompleted. Soon we'll all gather to talk about our day and praise the Lord. You don't want to miss that. Here, have a drink. You must be thirsty after all your hard work."

He held out a flask. Maxine took it obediently and drank deeply. She sighed, and the light faded from her eyes. Without another glance at Mrs. Entwhistle, she picked up her clippers and went back to work.

Emanuel patted Maxine's shoulder and whispered something in her ear. Then he turned to Mrs. Entwhistle.

"Is there anything else I can help you with?" he asked.

"Why won't you let Maxine go home?"

"Of course, she can go home any time she wants. She prefers to stay here."

Mrs. Entwhistle tried one more time. "Max, come on, let's go home and have some of your good soup. Martin misses you, and he's not being very nice to Roger. We all want you to come home."

But Maxine didn't even look up, so intent was she on her task. She clipped every twig as though it was a hair on the head of her favorite child. Mrs. Entwhistle gave up. Turning away, she bit back a scathing remark to Emanuel, who hadn't left her side. *Remember, you can catch more flies with honey than with vinegar*, her mother's voice said in her head.

"Well, it certainly does look like an interesting place," she said insincerely. "And everyone seems so happy and contented. That's a rare thing in today's world. I envy them."

"Do you?" Emanuel's voice held a challenge. "Then you may want to consider making what we call a learning visit. People come to learn what the Disciples are all about. We get to know them; they get to know us."

"What about my hard heart?" Mrs. Entwhistle asked, managing a tinkling little laugh that nearly choked her.

"We can soften that heart up in no time," Emanuel

said, joining in her laughter. His eyes crinkled appealingly. In that instant, she saw the charm he could turn on like a tap.

"I think I'd like to make a learning visit," Mrs. Entwhistle said, striving for just the right note of humility and curiosity even if it killed her. "When can I come back?"

~*~

First things first, Mrs. Entwhistle thought to herself. Before I do anything, I've got to talk to Pete.

She drove to his house and was gratified to see his government car parked in the driveway. Pete was in the back yard with the baby, Corrie, in a sling across his chest as he supervised the boys in the sandbox.

"No throwing sand!"

Mrs. Entwhistle smiled at the memory of all the little sand-throwers she'd been in charge of in her younger days. "Pete, I see you're busy, but can you spare me a moment?"

"Of course. Boys, who can build a sand castle that looks like one at the Magic Kingdom?" He'd taken his family to Disney World recently.

The boys fell to work earnestly, and Pete walked over to Mrs. Entwhistle. Corrie, her namesake and godchild, reached out her fat arms. Mrs. Entwhistle took her, inhaled a restorative breath of baby sweetness and turned with Pete to climb the steps to the deck. They settled themselves where they could keep the sandbox in sight. Mrs. Entwhistle nestled Corrie in her lap and let the baby smudge up her glasses.

"Remember I asked you to keep your ear to the ground about that new preacher in town?" Mrs. Entwhistle began. "Well, I've just been to see him. Maxine has joined his group, or church, or whatever the heck it is, and she's staying with them out at the old Jenkins place. I tried to get her to leave with me, but she wouldn't. She doesn't seem like herself; she's all glassy-eyed and hardly talks."

"That's not the Maxine we know and love," Pete said. "Maxine *always* talks."

"Yes, and just when she started to look a little brighter, that preacher—Emanuel, he calls himself— gave her something to drink out of a flask, and then she went right back to Zombie Land."

"I don't like the sound of this," Pete said. "Have you talked to the sheriff?"

"I called him when Max went missing, but later she was seen in town with the group and seemed all right. She's adult and fully *compos mentis* as far as the law is concerned. I'm worried sick, Pete."

"I'll be glad to investigate," Pete said, reaching over to squeeze Mrs. Entwhistle's hand.

"Yes, and I appreciate the offer, but you'd have to get permission or an assignment or something from your work, and file reports to a supervisor and such. It would have to go through official channels, and I can't wait on that. Maxine is in danger; I can feel it. You know how my spine tingles when I'm onto something? Well, it's about to tingle me to death."

"You're going out there, aren't you?" Pete sighed. "And it won't do any good for me to try to talk you out of it."

"I can't get her to leave until I know first-hand why she's stuck there. If I can gain Emanuel's confidence, I'll be able to figure it out. Maxine would do the same for me."

Pete shook his head, but he knew Mrs. Entwhistle. "Okay, let's think of the safest way for you to do it. How are you going to gain entrance?"

"I already told Emanuel I was interested in what he calls a learning visit. He invited me to come back whenever I'm ready and spend twenty-four hours with the Disciples."

"That's a long time. Could you arrange for a shorter visit?"

"I doubt it. Emanuel has everything scripted down to the last detail to work to his advantage."

"I'm concerned that the food and water may be drugged. I wouldn't want you to sample either one, but you couldn't go without eating or drinking for twenty-four hours."

"How about if I said I was on a special diet and took my own food?"

"Do you think Emanuel would go for it? If he's drugging the groceries in order to keep his followers in line, he wouldn't want to give up that control over you. He might make you put your food in a central kitchen where he could doctor it."

"How about if I said I was fasting as part of my learning visit, and then hid some energy bars and water bottles in my clothing?"

"I'm trying to visualize what kind of clothing that would take! And besides, doesn't he make everyone wear a white robe?"

"Just when they go out, I think. They all had on regular clothes today. My idea could work, Pete."

"Promise me this: you'll call and let me know when

you're going, and we'll arrange some kind of signal in case you need to be rescued. Will you do that?"

"Of course, I will, and thank you."

~*~

Mrs. Entwhistle went back to the Shady Rest Assisted Living Center carrying an armload of clothes, and she made her way straight to Jacinta's room.

"Jacinta, honey, I wonder if you'd like to be my investigative assistant."

"Your assistant? You mean like Nancy Drew and her friend, Bess?"

"Well, kind of like that. You have a special skill I need. You see, I'm going undercover, and I need to be able to hide food in my clothing."

Jacinta frowned. "You need clothing made of hides?"

Mrs. Entwhistle reminded herself that Jacinta couldn't hear well. "No, Jacinta," she roared, "I need pockets sewn into my clothes where I can hide food."

"Oh," Jacinta said, as if this were a common request. "Oh, of course."

"I know what a good seamstress you are. You've been sewing for people in this town for years. Do you still have your sewing machine?"

"No, I gave it to my daughter when I moved here. But there's a sewing machine in the craft room. Let me take a look at your clothes."

Mrs. Entwhistle handed over a pair of cargo pants she'd just bought at Wal-Mart and one of Floyd's heavy denim work shirts. She was glad now that she'd never cleared out all of Floyd's clothes after his death. Floyd would smile if he knew he was helping. First, he'd scold her for taking risks. Then he'd smile.

Jacinta turned both garments inside out and examined them carefully. "What kind of food?" she asked.

"Energy bars and something to drink. I'd need enough to get by for about twenty-four hours."

"Could you carry juice boxes instead of water bottles?"

"Sure, I guess."

"Okay."

Jacinta sat at the sewing machine and began. Sewing was something Mrs. Entwhistle never had gotten the hang of, and she watched respectfully as Jacinta bent over her work with focus and determination. Gone was the woman who couldn't hold a thought beyond her ailments. Jacinta had something meaningful to do.

Pockets appeared on the inside of Floyd's shirt and the cargo pants, just the right size to hide a flat juice box or an energy bar. Jacinta sewed eight inside pockets that were invisible when the garments were turned right side out. It took her no time at all.

"There," she said, squinting up at Mrs. Entwhistle. "That ought to do it. What are you going to do in these clothes?"

Mrs. Entwhistle wouldn't have revealed her mission to the old, scatterbrained Jacinta, but to the alert woman now before her, she said, "I'm going to infiltrate the Disciples of Holiness and find out what the heck that Emanuel guy is doing to people."

CHAPTER FOUR

Clem Dearing had a pain in his head that felt like it might split his brain in two, but he kept his hand under Jane's arm. He could feel her weakness as she tottered along beside him.

He and Jane went with the others into a large room. Folding chairs faced a table that held paper cups. When everyone was seated, Emanuel strode to the front of the room carrying a crystal pitcher in both hands. When he'd ceremoniously deposited the pitcher on the table, he began to speak.

"Disciples of Holiness! The Lord has called you to me for a very special reason. You are the point of the spear, chosen to carry forth His work into the community. You will bring in other souls, but first, you must prove yourselves worthy. The Lord looks down at our gathering, and He knows what is in your hearts. If any of you are holding back your complete trust in me, He knows. If any of you are reluctant to give of your bounty for our great work, He knows. If any of you are harboring thoughts that put yourselves and your loved ones first, He knows. Great will be his wrath if you do not submit your will to Him, for He will not tolerate disobedience. Fear Him, Disciples, and let that fear lead you to perfect obedience."

A few people squirmed in their chairs, but most stared expressionlessly at Emanuel. He began pouring liquid into the paper cups.

"Come now and drink of the Lord's pure Agua Vita, the water of life. It will cleanse your hearts and fit you for the work that is ahead. You." He pointed at Clem. "You come first."

Clem placed Jane's hand, which he'd been holding, in her lap. His knees cracked as he stood and walked forward. He knew Emanuel had been preaching to him. He'd tried to explain why he couldn't turn over their nest egg.

"Jane is fragile," he'd said, "and she forgets things. She needs the structure Shady Rest provides. I have to put her well-being first."

"Your care for your wife is commendable," Emanuel had said in his authoritative bass. "But remember, you will always have a home with me. You are among the chosen bedrock of the Disciples of Holiness. The Lord said of St. Peter, 'On this rock, I will build my church.' On rocks like you and Jane, I will build mine."

Clem tried to accept Emanuel's reassurance, but he was still worried. He admitted it to himself and then to Emanuel. "I'm not worthy to be a Disciple. My trust in you is not perfect."

"I know, my son, I see the dark cloud of worry hanging over your head. You are a work in progress, as we all are. Relax and give yourself to the process."

Now Clem was being called to the front of the gathering. He took a deep breath, trying to steel himself for whatever came next. If only his head wasn't throbbing. If only he could think more clearly.

Emanuel raised his voice. "I have chosen Clem to receive the Agua Vita first. Our brother, Clem, has been consumed by fears. He has been giving in to worry, but the Lord will restore him to us."

All eyes were on Clem as Emanuel handed him a cup. He drained it in two swallows. Almost immediately he felt better, as if he'd just had a restful night's sleep. He'd been worrying about an unimportant thing like handing over all his savings to the Disciples of Holiness, and now he saw how unnecessary worry was. He smiled broadly. Emanuel started clapping, and everyone obligingly patted their hands together.

Clem returned to his seat, where Jane looked at him questioningly. "I'm all right now," he told her. "Go up with the others and get a drink."

~*~

Maxine joined the line to the table. She, too, had a bad headache. Mixed with the pain was a nagging memory of seeing Cora. When had that been? It seemed like they'd been outdoors, and Maxine had been working. Cora mentioned Martin, but Maxine couldn't recall what she'd said. Something worrisome. She did remember Emanuel's words, repeated often: she, Maxine, was a force in the community and would lead others to Discipleship. That's what she must hang onto when everything got fuzzy. She couldn't imagine herself as the Lord's tool. Handing out those tracts in the town square had been just plain embarrassing. If only her head would stop hurting, maybe she'd be able to get her thoughts in order.

~*~

Rev. McGill was in line, too. He rejoiced in the certainty that he was in the right place at the right time. Emanuel had talked to him at length about his calling as a minister.

"Terry," he'd said, "think how close you came to doing harm to your congregants by leading them in the wrong direction. But now that you've been shown the right path, you can go back to your church and help them become Disciples of Holiness like yourself."

Emanuel said denominations didn't matter, church doctrines didn't matter and church leaders didn't matter. All that mattered was trusting in Emanuel to reveal the Lord's guidance. It was so simple, really. There was no need to wrestle with ethical questions or try to interpret difficult scriptures. He could skip the awkward home visits and depressing hospital calls where he never seemed to find the right words, all the weddings and funerals that gobbled up his free time. Rev. McGill felt guilty, but people and their everlasting problems had worn him down, sapped his faith, and made him long for solitude. Now he could relax; Emanuel would handle it. All he had to do was obey, and he'd be doing the Lord's work.

~*~

Carol Anne missed her job at the Busy Bee Diner, and it made her sad. She'd learned to go to Emanuel and ask for Agua Vita when the sadness became intense. In just a few minutes, she'd feel so much better. If only she could slip that water into the drinking glasses at the diner. The thought of all those sinful people being cleansed without even knowing it was something she often discussed with Emanuel. He said she'd been placed in a special position of service—and here she'd been secretly agreeing with her mother that she was wasting her talents as a waitress. It just showed how clear everything became when Emanuel explained it.

~*~

Gus Goodlet's brain fog was so pervasive he couldn't remember what he used to do. Something with animals, he thought. He'd met Emanuel in a way that was connected with animals, he almost recalled. Brief snapshots flashed through his mind: a paper-covered examining table holding a little dog—or cat, maybe? —Emanuel's commanding presence on the other side of the table. He'd accepted an invitation to visit this charismatic man, and he'd never gone back home.

Gus hadn't had a good friend since he was a kid. There'd been no time in vet school and no time after he was in solo practice. It was a relief to have a strong, wise father figure in his life. Emanuel said he'd help him become an influential community leader. Gus knew he could only accomplish that if Emanuel helped him every step of the way. How fortunate he was to have such a mentor.

Mrs. Entwhistle did some shopping, and then headed home to try on her outfit. She fitted juice boxes and energy bars into the hidden inner pockets. In the outside pockets of the cargo pants, she put items she didn't mind being found if she was searched. Tissues, chewing gum, Chapstick, things like that. She could offer up these mundane objects if she had to, while keeping her secret stash hidden.

The baggy trousers and Floyd's big shirt hung on her spare figure. She stood in front of the full-length mirror on the closet door eyeing herself up and down. *I resemble a scarecrow, but that's the look I'm going for. If Emanuel asks why I'm dressed like this, I'll tell him I'm wearing my work clothes so I can help with chores during my stay. He'll like that; he's big on people doing chores.*

She called Dex. "Honey, I need you and Lara to stay here at my house with Roger and Martin for a day and night. I wouldn't ask, I know you're busy getting ready to move to Washington, but it's important."

"Of course, Mrs. E.," Dex replied. "You know we'd do anything for you. When do you need us?"

"Tomorrow."

"We'll be there. What's going on?"

"It's Maxine. She's involved with Emanuel and the Disciples of Holiness. I found her living at the Jenkins place with a whole nest of 'em, and she wouldn't leave. She abandoned Martin, and you know how she loves that cat. There's something very wrong, and I'm going to find out what it is."

"How are you going to do that?" Dex asked. She could hear the eagerness in his voice. Next, he'd be wanting to join her.

"I'm going undercover," Mrs. Entwhistle said. "And no, Dex, you can't come. You're a married man now, about to start on your wonderful future. Besides, I've already established myself as an interested prospect with Emanuel."

"Do you think it could be dangerous?"

"Not if I'm careful. I have to find out how he convinces perfectly sane, logical people to abandon their lives and join him. I suspect drugs are involved, but I've planned how to avoid ingesting any myself." She told Dex about the secret pockets.

"I'm coming over. Don't change clothes yet; let me see if I can detect the pockets." Dex hung up.

In a short time, she heard his scooter turn into her driveway. She went out on the porch to greet him.

"Now just stand there in the bright sunlight and let me look at you," Dex said, bounding up the steps.

Mrs. Entwhistle turned in a slow circle. Dex narrowed his eyes.

"So far, so good," he said. "I can't see anything. Raise your arms."

She did.

"Now stoop down."

Jacinta had sewed snaps at the top of each pocket to keep the contents from sliding out. Mrs. Entwhistle heard a faint sloshing as the contents of the juice boxes shifted with her movement. She disguised it by coughing.

"Sit on this chair and lean back."

That was a problem. One of the square boxes hit right on her lumbar spine, and the sharp corners hurt. She sat bolt upright, her back not touching the chair.

"Okay, that won't work. Whatever's poking you in the back has to go," Dex said.

One less juice box. Oh, well, it couldn't be helped. Maybe she'd be able to sneak a drink of tap water when no one was looking. It would only be twenty-four hours, after all.

"I think you can pull it off," Dex said. "But you're going into a tricky situation. You have to convince Emanuel that you're sincere while finding out what he's up to."

They were interrupted by the arrival of Pete Peters, Deputy U.S. Marshall. He left his car door open, crossed the yard and bounded up the steps to join them on the porch.

"Is this your hidden stash outfit?" he said to Mrs. Entwhistle. "Let's take a look at it."

Pete examined her outfit carefully. He had her repeat the twirling, reaching and stooping exercises before declaring himself satisfied.

"It's still risky," he said. "Are you sure you want to go through with it?"

"Of course I don't. I'd much rather sit on the porch and have a cup of tea, but Maxine needs me. She'd do it for me."

"Okay, then let's set up some safeguards. Will you have your cell phone with you?"

"I'm not taking it. I'm sure it would be confiscated. Emanuel can't allow anyone to have unrestricted access to the outside world."

"Then we'll need some kind of signal in case you need help. I've been thinking about it. You won't be able to leave a note under a rock or tie a ribbon to a tree branch. You need something that doesn't require a recharger or an electrical connection, something that can be reliably used in daylight or darkness and won't alert Emanuel. Here's what I propose." Pete handed her a whistle.

"Don't you think Emanuel might become suspicious if I blast away on a whistle?" she asked.

"Try it."

She blew into the whistle, but heard nothing. She blew again, harder. A huge shape leaped from Pete's car and flew onto the porch. Mrs. Entwhistle could scarcely credit what she saw sitting before her: a one-hundred pound German shepherd dog, ears straight up, eyes intent.

Pete laughed at the expressions on her and Dex's faces. "Meet Axel. He's a retired police dog, but he still has his old skills. I borrowed him from one of my law-enforcement friends. Axel was his partner until he got too old for police work; then he became the family pet. He's going to be our signal detector. You'll carry the whistle in one of your hidden pockets. Axel and I will be camped near the Jenkins' farm, close enough for Axel to pick up the whistle sound. It's set at a frequency too high for human ears to detect, but he can hear it. If I see him alert, I'll know you're signaling me, and I'll respond."

"I'm going to be right there with Pete," Dex said.

"That's not necessary, Dex, you've got a lot going on right now," Pete protested, but Dex was having none of it.

"Nope, I've got nothing more important to do," he said in a tone that ended the debate. "Lara will stay at the house and take care of Martin and Roger, and I'll come with you."

"Well, I can't deny it would be good to have you. I'm doing this strictly as a private citizen, so I can't call the Marshall Service for backup. We don't know what we're up against with this guy. Thanks, Dex. Now, Mrs. Entwhistle, when are you going for your visit?"

"Emanuel said I don't need to make further arrangements, to just come on any day. So how about tomorrow?"

CHAPTER FIVE

Jacinta felt more alive than she'd felt in ages. She swallowed her morning pills absently, not even double-checking to make sure she was taking the right ones at precisely the right time. Her mind was filled with the adventure on which Mrs. Entwhistle was embarking. Undercover work! Jacinta had read every one of the Nancy Drew books in grade school, and, secretly, again as an adult. She dreamed of being a sleuth and uncovering mysteries. Because she was a natural follower, she'd identified most with Bess, the loyal side-kick. Cora Entwhistle was a perfect Nancy—fearless and daring.

Jacinta and Cora Entwhistle had gone through school together. They'd learned to read about Dick and Jane, write in cursive and memorize their multiplication tables; they'd played Red Rover at recess and swapped goodies from their home-packed lunches. As a little girl, Jacinta had wished for nothing more than to be as self-confident as her friend, Cora, but adolescence brought a parting of the ways. Jacinta was pretty and when they were seventeen, she was crowned Miss Corn Tassel. It turned her head, just as her mother said it would. From then on, Jacinta cared for nothing but having a date every Saturday night. Cora made A's and hung out with the brainy kids. She started dating Floyd during senior year and never looked at anyone else.

So they'd taken different paths, but stayed in touch as people in a small town do, whether they want to or not. Now Jacinta had a chance to get in on an adventure that might even be dangerous. Maybe she could come to Cora's aid if things didn't go well. Imagine: Jacinta to the rescue! The idea was irresistible. Oh, this was such an opportunity! Why had she ever thought she was too old to be useful? It's never too late—she'd heard Cora and Maxine say that a million times. Well, she was about to prove it.

Gus Goodlet was cutting the grass in the orchard when he received the message that Emanuel wanted to see him. He turned off the mower with a foreboding that maybe he'd done something wrong. He wished he could have a swig of Agua Vita for courage, but as it turned out, it wasn't needed after all.

"Gus, you're one of my best Disciples," Emanuel purred in his deep voice. "I think it's time for you to return to your life and spread the word of Discipleship."

"Uh, what was it that I used to do, you know, before, in real life?" Gus asked. He felt foolish, but he really couldn't remember.

Emanuel's brows drew together. "This is your real life now. You are a veterinarian, Gus, one in a unique position of trust. People look up to you; they respect your judgment. Soon you must return to your profession and use your influence to bring others to Discipleship. It's time for you to begin your reentry."

"I'm not sure I'm ready to leave yet." Panic made his voice shake.

"It is time," Emanuel repeated firmly. "You will not drink any Agua Vita from here on. Your head may hurt; if it does, tell me and I'll give you some aspirin. It's okay for you to rest—sleep if you can."

Gus nodded mutely, but he was sick at heart. *Why did things have to change? Why now, when he'd been feeling safe and worry-free?* He tried one last objection. "But my chores?"

"Don't worry about your chores; others will do them. You have a higher calling. That's why I chose you to be one of the first, the point of the spear. Remember?"

Emanuel was interrupted by a tap on the door announcing the presence of the runner. Every day, people had different tasks. The runner ran errands all day long, and today it was Maxine who stuck her head around the door.

"Someone to see you, Emanuel," she said. "A woman who wants to make a learning visit."

"Ah, Mrs. Entwhistle?"

"No. Not her. It's Jacinta." Maxine's flat voice expressed no surprise and no interest in the visitor. "I'll bring her."

~*~

Jacinta's sense of adventure and self-confidence faded as she walked into the room and met Emanuel's gaze. Maxine was acting like some kind of zombie, and as if that wasn't scary enough, now she faced a man whose eyes locked onto hers and wouldn't let her look away. It made her feel a little dizzy. Her steps faltered to a stop just inside the door.

"Greetings, my child. Do you wish to visit the Disciples of Holiness?" Emanuel rumbled.

"Well, I mean, I guess so," Jacinta stammered. "If it's all right. Just a quick visit, though."

"Our learning visits are twenty-four hours long," Emanuel said. "A full day and night are required for the experience to resonate and make sense to you. You will attend our gatherings, help with some of the easier tasks, eat and sleep in community. Only then can you judge for yourself whether being a Disciple is your calling."

"But I couldn't stay that long. I didn't tell anyone at Shady Rest that I would be gone overnight. They'll worry."

"Shady Rest Assisted Living Center? We have two members who came from there. Perhaps you would like to join them?"

"Oh? Someone from Shady Rest is here?" Jacinta made her eyes round and innocent. She figured he was talking about Clem and Jane Dearing, but she didn't let on. Really, she should have continued her drama studies after high school. Who knows what she could have become? Miss Corn Tassel might have been only the beginning instead of the high point of her life.

Emanuel could put on an act himself. He continued smoothly. "The Dearings have joined us. Do you know them?"

"Of course, I know Jane and Clem. I'd love to see them."

"Excellent. Maxine?"

Maxine lifted her eyes from the contemplation of her shoes. Her face was blank.

"Please take Jacinta to the kitchen and welcome her with a glass of Agua Vita. Then find Clem and Jane and leave her with them."

Obediently, Maxine took Jacinta's arm and steered her toward the door.

"But the Shady Rest?" Jacinta said over her shoulder. "Will you tell them where I am? I should get meal credits if I'm not there because I already paid for the whole month."

"Don't worry," Emanuel said tenderly. "I will see to everything. You are in my care now."

His face radiated such warmth that Jacinta imagined she could see a glowing aura of light around him. She kept looking back over her shoulder as she followed Maxine out of the room.

~*~

Emanuel stripped the white robe over his head and left it crumpled inside-out on the floor. The disciple on household duty would pick it up, wash and press it, and return it to his closet to hang beside the other pristine white robes. The polyester fabric was hot and itchy, but when he appeared draped in spotless white, it set him apart from ordinary people. The others weren't allowed to wear white robes unless they were in town on church business. Maybe when the money started coming in he'd order new everyday robes for the group. Some kind of cheap, dark fabric that wouldn't show the dirt. It would give the group more cohesion if they were all dressed alike every day.

He lost himself in delightful contemplation of all the things he'd do once the money tap was flowing. It would take a while; he knew that from past experience. He'd had to learn patience among many lessons, but he was an apt student. He knew how to draw in the influential members of a small town, how to make them vulnerable with drugs and brain-washing, groom them and then turn them back into the community to attract others. He knew how to shape the disciples' daily experiences to plant his message deeply into their heads.

Once he'd refined the drink and named it Agua Vita,

he'd certainly shortened that process. It was still a bit hit or miss; some Disciples became overdosed zombies, and some got splitting headaches when their dosage was insufficient. But once he got them regulated, their old worlds fell away and their new worlds began. Then he could etch his message in their empty minds with indelible ink. *Indelible think,* he laughed to himself.

Most importantly, he'd learned to disappear with the money just two steps ahead of the awakening. For he'd learned there was always an awakening. There would be a person who saw through him and raised the alarm. He thought of him or her—and most often it was a woman—as the community alarm clock. He fancied he had gotten good at identifying and outwitting her. But first, he enjoyed playing a little game of cat and mouse. The extra risk spiced up a gambit that was growing stale with repetition. Each time, he pushed the limit of his personal safety just a millimeter farther. Maybe this time he'd only be a step-and-a-half ahead of the law.

When Emanuel met Cora Entwhistle, he recognized her instantly. He knew an alarm clock when he saw one. She intended to nail him, and a shiver of excitement warned him she just might be the one to finally succeed. She would be a worthy adversary. Emanuel smiled in anticipation.

~*~

Mrs. Entwhistle drove Maxine's car up the long driveway to the Jenkins' house. The morning sparkled with the promise of a beautiful day. She took in the improvements made to the property since the Disciples of Holiness moved in and had to admit the old place looked much better. The grass was cut, beds were weeded and edged, and everything that could be painted wore a fresh coat of bright white. A number of Disciples were working on the barn, replacing rotted timbers and cutting down the weeds that had overgrown the barnyard. She parked beside some other cars and walked up the steps to the front door. It opened as she raised her hand to knock, and there stood Maxine.

"Max! I'm so glad to see you," Mrs. Entwhistle said, reaching out her arms for a hug.

But Maxine only nodded, her arms at her sides, then turned and walked back into the house. Mrs. Entwhistle followed, swallowing her hurt and disappointment at her old friend's unenthusiastic greeting.

Emanuel waited in his office which used to be the old farmhouse's front parlor, now fitted with a couple of bookcases and a desk. He rose when they entered.

"Ah, Mrs. Entwhistle," he said, with that appealing, crinkly smile. He wore a snowy white robe, setting off his dark hair, tanned skin and gleaming teeth.

The better to eat you with, Mrs. Entwhistle thought. Emanuel was a handsome man and knew exactly how to use his looks to his advantage, but it was wasted on her.

"How wonderful to have you visit us so promptly. I look forward to showing you around, but just now, I'm expecting a phone call. Maxine will take you to see where you'll be sleeping and get you settled in."

Again, Maxine turned on her heel and marched off with Mrs. Entwhistle hurrying behind her. She had hoped for the opportunity to catch Maxine alone, and it was happening sooner than she expected. If she could talk to Max, remind her of their friendship, remind her of home, then surely this evil spell would be lifted. In her head, she prepared what she'd say.

They went up a steep, enclosed staircase to the attic where about twenty narrow cots were arranged in rows. Maxine pointed at the bed nearest the door that was to be Mrs. Entwhistle's. Beside it stood a small table holding a pitcher and glass. Maxine couldn't look away from them.

"Max, are you thirsty? Help yourself," Mrs.

Entwhistle said. "Did you have breakfast? You don't look well."

"I've got such a headache." Maxine clutched her temples. "Agua Vita always makes it go away."

"Is that what's in the pitcher, Agua Vita? Then have some." She hated to use Maxine as a guinea pig, but it was important to see the effect of the water first-hand.

"We're not supposed to unless Emanuel says so."

"Well, I don't see him anywhere near, do you? For heaven's sake, Max, if your head hurts and the water helps, drink it." She poured a glass of water and held it out.

Maxine looked left and right, then grabbed the glass and chugged the contents. She stood still for a moment, then sighed and opened her eyes. They were glassy.

Mrs. Entwhistle watched her anxiously. "How are you feeling? Are you okay?"

"Okay now. Just real sleepy." Maxine was weaving on her feet. She sat down on the edge of Mrs. Entwhistle's bed. "Do you mind if I just...."

Maxine crumpled slowly, asleep before her head touched the pillow. Mrs. Entwhistle's rehearsed speeches were rendered useless by one glass of that darn water. There was some kind of drug in it, for sure. She picked up the pitcher, raised it to her face and sniffed; no odor and the liquid was clear. But whatever it was, it took effect quickly. Maxine was sleeping deeply. Mrs. Entwhistle studied her.

There were purple circles under Maxine's eyes and she'd definitely lost weight. Her beautiful white hair was carelessly brushed and needed a wash and set. Maxine's one vanity was her hair and it was shocking to see that she was neglecting it. She slept curled up with one hand under her cheek, breathing heavily.

Watching her, Mrs. Entwhistle was swept with a fury that turned her face scarlet and tightened her jaw. What was the point of drugging an elderly woman and keeping her captive? What possible gain could Emanuel expect to get from Maxine? Until she understood that, she'd be fighting blindfolded.

Follow the money. It's always about the money with someone like Emanuel.

.

CHAPTER SIX

"Caleb, where are my good shoes?" Booger asked his son.

Caleb looked up, surprised to see his parent dressed in going-to-town overalls, his round face clean-shaven and shining with soap and water. Booger was padding around in his sock feet poking ineffectually in corners and under tables for the missing shoes.

"Did you look in your closet?" Caleb asked.

"Well, durn, a'course I looked in my dang closet." Sometimes Booger couldn't believe he'd raised such a dope.

"Try the back porch. You might'a left 'em there when you came home from church last Sunday."

And that's where the shoes were, mighty oxfords with heavy laces that Booger put on and tied firmly in double knots. Then he clomped back to Caleb. "I'm ready now," he said.

"Ready for what?"

"Why, for you to take me to town."

"What for, Daddy? Do we need something at the store? I just got in groceries a couple days ago."

"No, it ain't the store. I aim to go see Cora Entwhistle."

"Now, Daddy, Miz Entwhistle don't seem too interested in having you visit."

"Mind your bidness, boy. Just git in the truck."

Booger rued the day he'd agreed to give up driving. After his heart attack, he'd been more amenable to suggestion than he'd ever been in his life, just out of sheer gratitude at still being around. That and the drugs they'd given him. He'd agreed then to give up his keys and turn the driving over to his son. But now he was himself again, and it was a royal pain in his backside to have to ask Caleb anytime he wanted to go somewhere.

As for Mrs. Entwhistle, well, he wasn't stupid; he knew she didn't take a shine to him right now. But

Booger possessed patience. He could wait. And meanwhile, he'd make sure she noticed him occasionally, just to keep his hand in.

He'd mulched her flower beds last fall while she and Maxine were off traipsing around God knows where. When the trees in his orchard were bearing, he dropped off cherries and peaches. And every few weeks he'd arrive unannounced at her door, standing mutely until she asked him to have a seat— on the porch if the weather was good, or in Floyd's old recliner in the living room if it wasn't. He'd stay for exactly half an hour, responding in monosyllables to her conversational gambits, which got more desperate as time passed. Floyd hadn't been much of talker, but Booger made him seem like a chatter-box.

At the end of thirty minutes he'd rise, nod solemnly and return to the car where Caleb read the newspaper while he waited for his father. Booger always had a feeling of a job well done after one of these visits. Let Caleb say what he would, Booger believed he was gaining ground in Mrs. Entwhistle's affections. It was worth the effort, too, because Cora Entwhistle was one in a million. She could be fierce as a wolverine and as independent as a hog on ice, but Booger didn't require a submissive little lady at this stage in his life. Mrs. Entwhistle got into trouble a lot, but she was kind-hearted, smart, and she could cook, too. Yes, she was worth some effort.

But today his knock on the door was answered by an unfamiliar young woman. "Yes, can I help you?" she asked pleasantly.

Roger peered around her ankles, not sure whether he should be barking or not. He didn't want to bark unnecessarily; at his age, it took too much effort.

Booger shuffled his feet and said, "I'm here to see Miz Entwhistle."

"Oh, she's not home right now. I'm Lara. She asked me to look after the pets while she's gone."

"Gone? Where's she off to now?"

A wary look came over Lara's face. "Uh, she's visiting friends, I believe. May I take your name and tell her you came by?"

"It's Booger, ma'am. Cora and me go way back."

"Oh, you know my husband, Dex Shofield. He and Mrs. Entwhistle investigated the wind farm scam for the newspaper."

"Yes, ma'am. Dex is a mighty fine young'un. Him and Cora done good."

"Well, I'll certainly tell Mrs. Entwhistle you were here. Good to meet you."

Booger was left standing on the porch looking at the closed door. Lara had been nice enough, but she wasn't going to give him any information about Cora's whereabouts, that was obvious. He returned to the car deep in thought. He knew a place you could be sure of finding out anything that was happening in a fifty-mile radius.

"Caleb, I have a taste for one of them donuts at the Busy Bee. Take me over there, son."

~*~

It was a hot morning, and Mrs. Entwhistle was too warm in her voluminous outfit. The juice boxes would be body temperature and the chocolate chips in the energy bars would be melted, but there was no help for it. She'd left Maxine asleep on her cot, gone back downstairs and volunteered to work in the barn. Now she was slapping white-wash on an ancient horse stall. The sun shone down through the many holes in the roof, making the dust motes sparkle and raising the temperature to an even more uncomfortable level. She wished she could get at one of those juice boxes right now, warm or not, but she was surrounded by other workers who would notice if she went digging through her clothing.

She knew most of the folks by name, but found them inexplicably reluctant to have a conversation. Her questions were met with blank stares or noncommittal smiles. Why were they here? How had they been convinced to abandon their lives, even temporarily, to live and work on the old Jenkins place? What had Emanuel done to convince them? It beggared the imagination. Mrs. Entwhistle painted on, pausing to wipe the sweat that was running into her eyes. When a member of the day's kitchen crew passed out paper cups of liquid, she salivated, but said, "No, thank you." She couldn't take a chance of being drugged.

She painted the last corner of her assigned space and levered herself to her feet. "I'll just wash my brush at the hose," she said. While she was at it, she sneaked a long drink which tasted like plastic, but was delicious nonetheless. Her fellow workers didn't seem to be keeping track of her, so she decided to slip away and have a private look around.

Everywhere she went there was industry—cleaning, sweeping, painting, mowing, trimming and digging. When did Emanuel do his brain-washing? People couldn't be kept in place forever with drugged water and busy work.

The answer to that question came almost immediately when the musical tones of a gong floated through the still air. Emanuel stood on the front porch striking a hammered brass circle with a mallet. Workers dropped their tools and started walking toward the house. Mrs. Entwhistle joined them as they seated themselves in a semi-circle around the porch steps. Watching the middle-aged or older people lower themselves gingerly to the ground, she wondered how they'd manage getting up again. Emanuel might have to pull off a real miracle to make that happen.

She saw Clem and Jane Dearing, Dr. Goodlet, Roger's vet—that explained why he was AWOL from his office—Carol Anne from the Busy Bee Diner, Rev. McGill, Maxine, and, oh, for heaven's sake! Jacinta. What in the world was she doing here? It would be just like her to ask Emanuel if he'd care to see the ingenious pockets she'd sewn in Mrs. Entwhistle's clothes. She cursed herself for letting Jacinta know she was investigating the Disciples of Holiness.

Emanuel was speaking. His rumbling bass voice and piercing eyes seemed to hold the little congregation spell-bound. No one looked away, checked the time or stirred. All eyes were on the white-robed figure who addressed them from the porch steps.

Mrs. Entwhistle half-listened to what she considered boiler-plate exhortations about obedience, enlightenment and proselytizing. Surely, he'd said all this a thousand times before—he even sounded a bit bored—but his audience drank it in. Her ears perked up when Emanuel started in on his idea of discipleship.

"Do you have enough worldly goods to supply your needs? Do you have, in fact, more than you need? The Lord loveth a cheerful giver. As you bring more and more people into the Disciples of Holiness fellowship, our needs will increase as we seek to feed, house and teach the new converts. Ask yourself what you can give to help our holy cause. Can you give your savings? Can you give your house, your car? Do you trust the Lord to supply your needs?"

One by one, the Disciples struggled to their feet to pledge what they had. Clem Dearing said he'd withdraw all the funds from his IRA because he and Jane wouldn't need it now that they were permanent residents of the church. Dr. Goodlet said he didn't have much money yet, but he promised half of his income from his veterinary practice.

"And you will be bringing us new souls, Gus. Well done." Emanuel beamed a radiant smile at him. The young vet turned as pink as a schoolboy.

Rev. McGill spoke in his ringing pulpit voice of how he would direct a portion of the offerings taken at his church to the Disciples of Holiness. He looked at

Emanuel for his own personal "attaboy," but instead he was met with narrowed eyes and contracted brow.

"A portion?" Emanuel thundered. "Brother McGill." Heavy sigh. "Obviously, you have not absorbed my message. I am not angry, only disappointed. Disappointed!"

The reverend dropped back onto the grass like he'd been shot. His companions sent him surreptitious looks of sympathy. They didn't exactly know what he was in for now, but they wanted no part of it.

Then Emanuel pointed at Maxine. Mrs. Entwhistle held her breath. What would her friend offer? Maxine owned a house and car and had enough savings to live comfortably, if modestly, in retirement. She didn't have a lot of extra.

Mrs. Entwhistle knew all about Maxine's loving, generous heart so she shouldn't have been surprised, but still, she could hardly believe her ears when Maxine pledged it all—everything she owned—to Emanuel. Not to the so-called church; to the man himself. Emanuel descended from his place on the porch steps to give her a long, warm hug.

"Bless you, sister! Did you all hear that?" He turned a radiant face to the others. "Our sister, Maxine, has given everything she has. The widow's mite! Think about that as you decide what your gift will be. Maxine, we'll go to town and take care of the legalities just as soon as possible. Don't fear for the future; you'll always have a home with me."

Like hell! Mrs. Entwhistle thought profanely. She didn't swear often, but this was a swearing occasion if ever there was one. Thank goodness she'd found Maxine in time. She fully intended that Max would be back home detoxing from that nasty water by tomorrow this time.

~*~

Caleb watched Booger absorb donuts and gossip at the Busy Bee Diner. He'd never have imagined his taciturn father could be so good at schmoozing, but it seemed the old man could do it if he wanted to.

"So, what's been going on around town?" Booger asked his fellow counter-sitters.

There was an excited recital of events that seemed to be all about the new preacher in town, Emanuel and the Disciples of Holiness. People talked over each other with tales of the revitalized Jenkins farm and names of the well-known town citizens who had joined the new church.

"Is it mostly the rich folks out there?" Booger asked.

"No siree, it's just about anybody you could think of. Maxine—you remember her, in our class at school? Well, she's joined. She was in the square passing out tracts, all dressed up in a white robe. She acted like she didn't recognize me, and I've known Maxine since we were in Cradle Roll Sunday School together. And Rev. McGill! He's got his own church, and you'd think one would be enough for anybody, but he didn't even tell Rita where he was going. Just didn't show up in the church office one morning."

Hmmm. If Maxine was at the Jenkins place, Booger knew it was a good bet that Cora Entwhistle was there, too.

"What's this Emanuel's angle?" he asked bluntly. "I reckon he's gettin' something fer hisself. Never knew a preacher who didn't."

Heads were shaken and lips were pursed as people speculated. "I hear he's going to hold a big tent meeting out there tonight," one said. "I'm planning to go, just to see what's what." There was a chorus of agreement.

Booger slid off his stool and jerked his head toward the door. "C'mon, Caleb. I got one more stop to make."

~*~

Caleb drove his father slowly past the Jenkins farm. They peered down the long lane, but there wasn't much to see from the road.

"Do you want me to drive to the house?" Caleb asked.

"No, son," Booger said, "go on by and take the next left. Go slow so there ain't a big cloud of dust."

The Jenkins farm lay within a perfectly square four-mile tract of land. It was possible to drive the circumference of the farm on gravel roads, but almost impossible not to raise an obscuring powder. Caleb crept along at twenty-five miles per hour. As they turned at the last four-way stop, they saw a giant tent being erected in a field adjacent to the farm-house. Caleb pulled to a stop beside the road.

The canvas lay huddled on the ground, rising as men walked the tent poles upright. When the poles were in place, they hammered stakes around the periphery, grabbed ropes dangling from the canvas, and began tying it down. They were directed in their work by a tall figure in a white robe that flapped around his legs as he strode about, yelling orders. He didn't seem to be doing any of the actual work himself.

"Wish I'd a brought my spy-glass," Booger muttered.

"I guess that guy in the white nightshirt is the boss. Like to get a good look at him."

At that moment, the white-robed figure turned and peered their way. His head came up, and he pointed. All the workers looked, and a couple of them waved, having recognized Booger's truck.

"Time to go, Caleb," Booger said. "I've seen all I need to."

CHAPTER SEVEN

Maxine hadn't recognized the man on her doorstep and that was unusual in the small town where she'd lived all her life. She'd swung open the door with a welcoming smile, because he had to be a friend she just hadn't met yet. Maybe a neighbor's relative come for a visit, maybe a new resident. Whoever he was, she'd made him welcome, and when he introduced himself as a preacher starting a new church, she'd been delighted.

"Come in, come in," she'd said, ushering him into the living room. "I'll just get us a cup of tea, shall I? We can have a good talk. I'm Maxine, and what did you say your name is again?"

"I am Emanuel," the stranger said, looking deep into Maxine's eyes and smiling so warmly she had to smile back. "I'd love a cup of tea."

Maxine got out her best china, rinsing the cups and saucers in hot water to make sure they were pristine, warming and then filling the matching teapot with English Breakfast tea. She refreshed homemade oatmeal cookies in the microwave, arranged them on a plate with a lace paper doily and carried it all on a tray into the living room.

Emanuel was examining the family pictures and books in the bookcases that lined her walls. "Is this your daughter?" he'd asked, holding a framed photograph.

"Yes, that's my Geraldine."

"Beautiful girl; she looks like her mama. Does she live close by? Do you see her often?"

"No, she's all the way over in Australia. It's a big trip, but I did go once. She's come home a couple of times, but it's really expensive and she's working, so it's hard to get time off."

"So far away. You're a widow, aren't you? You must get lonely, living by yourself here in this house."

Emanuel had looked so sympathetic that Maxine felt he really cared. "Of course, I miss my late husband, but I don't think of being lonely because I've always lived here, and I know everyone. And I have my dear friend, Cora. She's like a sister to me. And of course, there's Martin, my cat."

On cue, Martin strolled into the room waving his tail. When he saw a stranger, he stopped in his tracks and flattened to the floor with his ears back. He and Emanuel eyed each other warily.

"Kitty, kitty," Emanuel said half-heartedly. It was plain he wasn't a cat person.

Martin hissed, wheeled and made a speedy exit. Maxine apologized. "He's not used to strangers," she said. "And cats—they're not always friendly. I'm sorry he hissed at you."

"No problem, my dear lady. Now tell me about yourself while we drink this delicious tea."

Maxine had needed no further invitation to launch into the tale of her recent trip on Route 66 with her friend, Cora. It took quite a long time to tell, what with all the sidebars and explanations. At one point, the phone rang, and she'd excused herself to answer it, stepping into the kitchen. Turned out to be a sales call, but it took her a minute to excuse herself politely. No matter how often Mrs. Entwhistle told her to "just hang up, for cryin' out loud," Maxine couldn't do it.

When Maxine tried to recall what happened after that, she drew a blank. The last thing she remembered was raising her teacup and drinking. Her next memory was waking up in the attic dorm with a hammering headache.

Sometimes Maxine dimly sensed that something was very wrong with her. That realization came with the headaches, but the pain drove away all efforts to figure it out. There had been a moment when her old friend's face and voice had stirred a stab of homesickness. It faded after she drank the water. Agua Vita. Emanuel said it meant Water of Life. Maxine had learned to crave it for the irresistible sleep it brought.

Maxine woke with a start and stumbled to her feet. Her hair was stuck to her face and her teeth felt like they wore little felt socks. Please, please let Emanuel not notice she'd sneaked an extra drink of Agua Vita and fallen asleep when she was supposed to be keeping tabs on Mrs. Entwhistle. She'd never seen Emanuel angry, but she knew instinctively she didn't want to.

Cora being here complicated everything. Maxine guessed she should be excited about the chance to convert her best friend, but the thought was as flat as a stale Co'Cola. She couldn't summon energy for anything. She slumped on the edge of the cot and tried to think what to do next. Mrs. Entwhistle's sudden appearance made her jump.

"Where have you been?" Maxine asked.

"Oh, just looking around a bit. I didn't meet anyone. Don't worry, you needed that little snooze, and I won't tell," Mrs. Entwhistle replied. "What do you say we go for a walk? I'd love to see more of the grounds."

Maxine agreed because it was easier to go than to say no. Mrs. Entwhistle headed to the orchard at the side of the house. Once they were within the shelter of the old apple trees, Mrs. Entwhistle stopped walking and took Maxine's arm.

"Now then, Max, tell me about this place and about Emanuel. Why are you here?"

"Well, Emanuel... I guess he must have said to come, I don't really remember."

"How did you meet him?"

"He came to visit me."

"And you asked him in and made tea, didn't you?"

"I think so, yes. I remember serving tea. Then I woke up here. This is a good place, a wonderful place." Maxine's voice was a monotone.

"What's wonderful about it?" Mrs. Entwhistle asked. She genuinely wanted to know.

"Uh, the Disciples of Holiness are called to be the point of the spear. We are blessed to be able to be in the vanguard of this wonderful movement. Together, we will save the world." Maxine could have been reading a hostage note for the cameras.

"I know that's what you've been programmed to say. But what do *you* think?"

"That *is* what I think. Isn't it?" Maxine said. She sounded dubious.

"What about when your head hurts? Do you still think so then?"

"No, then I have bad thoughts about leaving."

"Why don't you?"

"Emanuel gives me Agua Vita, and I feel so much better. Then I don't want to go away anymore. I'm safe here. I'll always have a home with him."

"Max, you won't! Think, now. Try hard to think with me. Emanuel isn't what he appears to be. He's a charlatan, an Elmer Gantry. He's trying to get as much money out of as many people as he can, and then he'll move on. Chances are he's done this many times before. Once he's fleeced everyone, he'll be gone and you'll be left sitting here with no home to go back to, no car and no savings."

Maxine looked troubled. She stopped and turned to search Mrs. Entwhistle's face. "Cora, how do you know?"

"Because my brain works, Max. I'm not drinking drugged water. You need to break free of this man's hold on you. I'm here to help you, to take you home again."

"I don't think you should be talking like this," Maxine said, looking around to see if anyone could have heard. "Emanuel would be very angry if he knew."

"What happens when he's angry?"

"I don't know." Maxine looked frightened. "But I think it's pretty bad. I need to go back to the house."

"Don't go. I won't say anything more about it."

But it was too late. Maxine turned and walked away, pausing to steady herself on a tree trunk.

~*~

As it turned out, Carol Anne was the first one to leave. Gus Goodlet was still getting his things together when Emanuel beckoned to Carol Anne and said it was time. She climbed into the car without protest, rode silently to her apartment, got dressed in her waitress uniform, then walked back into the Busy Bee Diner as if she'd never been gone. She ignored the angry mutterings of Herve', grabbed her order pad and went to work.

Carol Anne looked the same, but she seemed different. She took orders without the usual chit-chat about politics or literature. Her regulars looked at each other with raised eyebrows, but they concluded among themselves that Carol Anne was having a hard time getting back into the swing of things after her week off.

As the afternoon wore on and Carol Anne fell into the familiar routine, she felt more and more like herself. When she thought about staying out at the old Jenkins place with a random bunch of people, she wondered what she'd been thinking. She vaguely remembered she was supposed to be talking to her customers about joining the Disciples of Holiness, but she couldn't do it. She'd feel ridiculous. The whole experience seemed like it had happened to someone else. Her shift was almost over when Emanuel came in to get her.

He wasn't wearing his robe. Today he was dressed in jeans and a polo shirt like just about every other man in the place. He took a seat at one of Carol Anne's tables and waited for her to come over.

"How's it going?" he asked easily. "Creating any interest in our church?"

Carol Anne felt her face grow hot. She looked down at her order pad. "Um, not really, no. What can I get you?"

"I've come to take you home," Emanuel said, smiling his trademark smile. "And I've brought you a treat— a drink of Agua Vita. Figured you'd need it after a hard day's work." He showed her the flask he carried.

"No, thank you. No," Carol Anne said firmly. "That stuff makes me sleepy."

Emanuel's eyebrows rose. "Carol Anne, I think maybe I sent you back into the world too soon." He sounded sincerely concerned. "Let me take you back to the farm with me and you can spend a few more days in rest and fellowship."

"Nope, I'm not interested in doing that."

"Not even for me?"

Emanuel layered on the crinkly smile and warm eyes, but Carol Anne backed up a couple of steps.

He changed tactics. "Carol Ann, I command you to return with me."

His booming voice turned several heads. Carol Ann looked around nervously.

"Look, I'm working. I've got an order up. I can't stand here talking."

And she was gone.

Emanuel stood and stalked out the door. Carol Anne's defection was the first chink in his armor, and it increased his sense of urgency. He'd hoped she could interest some of her customers in visiting by slipping some Agua Vita into their glasses. Then he'd swoop in for more persuasion and before they knew what hit them, they'd be at the farm. The water was a shortcut that saved a lot of time. He hated waiting around while people dithered. Now that plan was shot. Cursing, he drove back to the farm.

The first person he saw after he'd parked the car was Mrs. Entwhistle. She was walking Maxine into the orchard.

He slipped behind the women and followed discretely. He could hear every word of their conversation and nodded with satisfaction when Maxine broke away and returned to the house. That was one disciple he'd nailed down. He stepped into the path where Mrs. Entwhistle stood looking after

Maxine.

"Good morning, sister. Are you finding your time with us enlightening? Do you have any questions I could answer?"

Mrs. Entwhistle started. She hadn't known Emanuel was anywhere nearby. The last she'd seen of him, he'd been driving Carol Anne toward town in Clem Dearing's car. She wondered how much he'd heard.

"It's a beautiful day," she said noncommittally. "I'm learning a lot."

"I noticed you didn't eat lunch. It's almost time for our evening meal. May I escort you to the dining room?"

"I'm fasting as part of my learning experience." Mrs. Entwhistle had rehearsed that lie and it came out glibly.

"Fasting is not recommended, but, of course, you may fast if you wish. It's important that you keep hydrated, however. Our Agua Vita is a vital part of the Disciples of Holiness experience. Surely your fasting doesn't preclude drinking water."

Emanuel's smile didn't reach his eyes as he held out his flask.

"No thanks. I find I experience the benefits of the fast

more fully if I limit water intake as well."

Emanuel was too much of a pro to tip his hand by insisting. "Let's walk and talk then, shall we?"

He took Mrs. Entwhistle's arm and drew it through his. He began walking in the direction of the tent that now stood in the pasture closest to the house.

"My, what a large tent," Mrs. Entwhistle said. "How many people does it hold?"

"Exactly the right number," Emanuel said. "Tonight, it will be full of souls seeking redemption. Don't you want to be one of the Disciples and welcomes them?"

"I haven't made up my mind yet about becoming a Disciple. Tomorrow morning when my twenty-four hour visit is over, I'll evaluate my experience and make a decision. I'll be watching how the tent meeting goes, and I hope it brings you everything you deserve."

Emanuel smiled. She was a sharp old gal, this one. She'd managed to extricate her arm from his and walked along matching him stride for stride. Their height was equal, so she didn't have to look up at him.

"Of course, you know you are free to leave any time

you wish, even though your twenty-four hours aren't up. Like right now, if you choose," Emanuel said.

"I wouldn't dream of leaving early. My learning experience wouldn't be complete. I want to be sure I know exactly how to describe the Disciples of Holiness to others."

"Your friend, Maxine, is well versed in our doctrine. She can help you."

"Yes, I realize that. I'd love to have some exclusive study time with her. I feel sure she could make it all clear to me. We're old friends, you know."

"I find it's best if our visitors remain in community. Maxine has duties and it's important that she learn to focus on them."

"Maxine is an adult. She's old enough to know where her duty lies." Mrs. Entwhistle couldn't help it; her voice shook with anger. She took a deep breath. She couldn't lose her cool now, no matter how much this polished manipulator baited her.

"Ah!" Emanuel sounded amused. "I'm certain that she does. And isn't it wonderful that, even at her advanced age, she is able to learn obedience? We should all cultivate that quality."

"I find obedience greatly over-rated compared to logical thinking. If you'll forgive me for saying so, I haven't seen much logical thinking in your group."

"'What does the brain matter compared with the heart?'" Emanuel quoted.

"Virginia Woolf. I've read **Mrs. Dalloway**, but I'm surprised you have."

Emanuel shrugged. "I'm always interested in what wise women have to say. Now it's time for us to join the others for the evening meal. Even if you choose not to eat, I must insist that you at least sit with us for the fellowship."

"I wouldn't miss it for the world," Mrs. Entwhistle said grimly.

CHAPTER EIGHT

"I'm not gonna change clothes," Booger told Caleb, "because we're goin' out again tonight."

"Tonight?" Caleb could not have been more astonished. It was his father's unshakeable habit to be tucked in bed by eight p.m. every night. "Out? Late?"

"Yep. We're goin' to that tent meetin' the new preacher is havin'."

"That don't sound like something you'd normally do," Caleb observed.

"These ain't normal times. Somethin' is goin' on at the Jenkins place, and I don't like the sounds of it. I believe Cora and Maxine are mixed up in it, and I aim to be there in case I'm needed."

"What could *you* do, Daddy?"

"What d'ya mean, what could I do? I'm not so stove-up and decrepit that I couldn't help. And besides, you'll be there, too."

"Couldn't I just wait in the car?"

"No, son. You're comin' in with me. Now I want you to get my Colt down from the cupboard."

Caleb's eyes widened. Getting the Colt meant this was serious business indeed. It was an old-fashioned weapon passed down through the family, never called upon except in direst emergencies. Usually Booger counted on his shotgun, which stood in its place beside the front door. Booger saw him look at it.

"Cain't very well tote a shotgun into a meetin'," he said. "But I don't aim to go unarmed, not with this bad feelin' I got."

The old revolver had long ago been wrapped in an oily rag and deposited on the top shelf of the breakfront. There it had rested for as long as Caleb could remember. The ammunition for it was equally ancient. The gun might fire, or it might blow up. Caleb suspected he was in for a very interesting evening.

~*~

The Rev. Terrence McGill's knees were shaking as he stood before Emanuel. He'd incurred the leader's wrath, and he still wasn't sure why.

"So, Terry, you'll be dedicating a *portion* of your church's offerings to the Disciples of Holiness?" Emanuel said in a silky voice.

"Well, yes, I can't do more than that right off the bat. The congregation gets an accounting of where their offerings go. I'm not sure I can even get away with giving a portion, but I'll disguise it as Foreign Missions until I can get people to see the light." He smiled ingratiatingly. "*Your* light, Emanuel."

Emanuel was not beguiled. "The Disciples' work must not wait. I expect you to turn over the entire offering to me. At once."

"I can't do that!"

Rev. McGill looked agonized, and Emanuel saw that he'd pushed him too far. But he didn't have time to wait around while this sniveling preacher sweet-talked his congregation into compliance. Without the aid of Agua Vita, it could take a while. Emanuel felt a tightening in his chest. This gig was almost up. He had to collect as much cash as he could in a hurry.

"Tonight at the tent meeting, I want you to get up and give your testimony about what you've learned as a Disciple. Members of your flock will no doubt be there, and it will soften their hearts."

"Might it be a bit too soon?" Rev. McGill said hesitantly. "My congregation may need more time to prepare themselves for such a change in their pastor's teaching."

"Your congregation must be led to the living water. You are their shepherd. It's your duty to lead them. Tonight, you will make a start."

The rebuke was delivered in Emanuel's deepest, most authoritative voice. He allowed displeasure to show in the gaze he focused on the hapless Rev. McGill, who looked like he wanted to throw up. When Emanuel thought the reverend was just the right shade of green, he made a show of relenting and poured a glass of water from the pitcher on his desk.

"Here, Terry," he said, "drink. You'll feel better in a minute. Then you can get started on preparing your testimony for tonight."

~*~

Clem couldn't get Jane to stop crying. "I just want to go home," she sobbed.

"But we *are* home, honey," Clem said, patting her narrow back. "This is where we live now."

"No! We live at Shady Rest. I want to sleep in my own bed and eat meals with our friends, and—oh, my head hurts so bad, Clem."

"You need to drink more. Maybe you're a little dehydrated. Let me go ask Emanuel if you can have an extra glass of Agua Vita. That'll fix you right up. Hang on, honey, I'll be back in a jiffy."

When he returned with a brimming glass, Jane drank eagerly. "Ah, that's better. Maybe you're right, maybe I was de— dehydrolized."

Jane's eyes rolled up in her head. Clem lowered her carefully to her cot and tucked a sheet over her. She'd sleep now, and when she awoke she'd be okay. Clem drained the rest of her glass. He felt a headache coming on, himself. That wouldn't do. Tonight would be a big event for the Disciples—their first outreach meeting to the community. He hoped the big tent would be packed with his friends and neighbors so he could tell them what he'd found. He wasn't sure exactly what he'd say, but Emanuel would be briefing them at dinner.

Gus Goodlet didn't want to wear his white doctor's

coat to the meeting. "I only wear it at the clinic when I'm seeing patients," he explained to Emanuel. "I'd feel silly wearing it to a church service."

"Ah, but Gus, you must look familiar to the folks tonight. They see you in that white coat, and they remember that you are a professional man, an educated man whom they trust. That's the message you want to convey, that's what will get them to loosen their purse strings and give to our work."

"Well, I'd really rather not..." Gus began, but he stopped when he saw Emanuel's eyes flash.

"You will obey me, Gus Goodlet!" Emanuel roared.

Gus felt as though a mighty wind had blown him backward. "Yes, of course, I will obey, Emanuel. Forgive me for questioning you," he stammered. Feeling silly was nothing compared to feeling Emanuel's wrath.

~*~

"Carol Anne, you going out to the tent meeting tonight?" one of the regulars at the Busy Bee Diner asked.

"Nope."

"I saw you talking to the preacher earlier. Aren't you curious about those folks?"

"Not anymore."

"You should come, though. Sounds like everybody will be there."

"Let me give you some free advice. If you go, don't drink the water."

"Why not? Is the well contaminated?"

"You could say that. Just don't drink it, I'm telling you."

Customers exchanged looks and shrugged. Carol Anne sure was grumpy since she'd had her week off. Vacations apparently didn't agree with her. And she seemed to know something about the new preacher that she wasn't telling. All the more reason to go to the tent meeting and see for themselves.

~*~

Maxine and Mrs. Entwhistle were shelling peas for dinner in the communal kitchen. Max looked up nervously when Emanuel approached.

"Maxine, you are truly among the blessed for your selfless donation to the Disciples. Tomorrow I want you to go to the bank and withdraw your savings."

"But how will I get there? I don't have my car."

"I will take you myself, but I won't go in with you. That might raise questions we don't have time, er, we don't need to deal with now. After all, it is your money, and you are free to do as you wish with it. We'll rehearse what you're going to say."

"I'll take her," Mrs. Entwhistle offered quickly. "I'm driving Maxine's car anyway, so I might as well."

"No. I will take her," Emanuel said, smiling into Mrs. Entwhistle's face. "From now on, I'll be assisting her with her business matters."

"Then you should know that aside from Social Security, she has only a small savings account. Most of her money is in CDs. She'll have to pay a penalty if she withdraws it. She has an annuity, but it will take a while to liquidate it, and it will take months to sell her house," Mrs. Entwhistle said, smiling right back.

"The Lord will understand," he said, "and meanwhile, we'll just get as much cash as we can to further His work."

Mrs. Entwhistle smiled more broadly. *Wait until Mr. Dansinger at the bank hears about this.* That was the beauty of a small town. The banker had been in Maxine's Sunday School class when he was a boy and had loved her like a mother ever since. Mrs. Entwhistle had asked for and received his help before when Maxine was ready to drain her bank account to help a bogus Nigerian prince. She had no doubt Mr. Dansinger would come through again.

CHAPTER NINE

Jacinta had been told the gong would announce dinner, and she waited on the front porch. Emanuel had hardly picked up the mallet before Jacinta whisked through the front door and made for the dining room.

Actually, the group ate in two rooms. The dining room wasn't big enough to hold all the Disciples, so the big pine kitchen table was pressed into service. Jacinta saw Mrs. Entwhistle and Maxine there and plopped herself down beside them.

"I've had the most amazing day!" she exclaimed in the loud voice of the hearing-impaired. "I'm so glad I came to visit. I just never would have believed there was such a place as this in our little town. And the water! Well, it will sure cure whatever ails you. I was worried about something when I got here, but darned if I can even remember what it was."

The food was brought to the table in big dishes. It seemed to be some kind of stew. There were limp carrots and greenish-looking potatoes along with stringy meat in glutinous gravy. Mrs. Entwhistle had sneaked one of her energy bars and a juice box just a few minutes earlier. She waved the dish past.

Maxine pushed the stew around on her plate, but drank her water with more enthusiasm. Any time a glass was half-full, a server topped it up. The conversation around the table grew more slurred and spasmodic, until finally everyone just sat staring ahead in silence.

Emanuel made the rounds, talking to each diner. When he approached Mrs. Entwhistle, Jacinta came to life.

"Oh, Reverend Emanuel, have you met my friend, Mrs. Entwhistle? I guess you have, since she's here. She's visiting, like me. Well, it was her idea; I just decided to come, too. Did she show you what I made for her? Ow!" She turned to Mrs. Entwhistle indignantly. "What'd you do that for?"

"Shut up, Jacinta," Mrs. Entwhistle hissed out of the side of her mouth. "Shut up right now."

Jacinta shut up. It was scary when Mrs. Entwhistle took that tone. She rubbed her instep and told herself that she'd meant no harm, she'd just been going to tell Emanuel about the—*ooooh!* Jacinta got the giggles when she realized she'd been about to tell him about the secret pockets. She couldn't stop laughing, even when Mrs. Entwhistle shot her a disgusted look. She covered her face with her paper napkin, shoulders shaking.

"What's so funny?" Emanuel asked. "Share it with all of us."

Jacinta thought he sounded like her sixth-grade teacher, who used to say the same thing when she got the giggles at school, and that made her laugh even more. Her awe of Emanuel was swamped by the Agua Vita in her system.

"Jacinta is nervous about being here," Mrs. Entwhistle said. "She feels a lot of pressure to conform and it's got her upset. She tends to giggle when she's upset."

"Is that right, Jacinta?"

She nodded helplessly. "I guess so. Whatever Cora says."

"I see. Whatever Cora says. Well, we'll have to get Cora saying the right things then, won't we?"

Emanuel moved on with a swish of his white robe. Gradually, Jacinta settled down. Then her chin dropped to her chest. Pushing her plate aside, she laid her head on the table and was instantly asleep. This elicited no surprised comments from her table-mates, some of whom were slumped in their chairs, also asleep. Maxine yawned widely, forgetting to cover her mouth. Mrs. Entwhistle shook her arm.

"Stay awake, Max," she whispered. "You're going to need to have your wits about you tonight."

When the server came around with the pitcher of water, Mrs. Entwhistle put her hand over Maxine's glass. "No more for her, thank you." Her tone brooked no argument.

~*~

The fragrance of crushed grass and sun-warmed canvas filled the tent. All kinds of seating had been set up—folding chairs, benches, lawn chairs and even kitchen stools faced a raised wooden platform. People were already filing in and more cars were parking alongside the road. The Disciples were seated on the platform. They'd been given white robes to wear, and most of them were awake now. They glanced at each other uneasily and rubbed their eyes. Was this real life or a dream? Were they really sitting in front of their friends and neighbors in a tent in a field? They stirred in relief when Emanuel turned his back on the assembling audience and spoke confidentially to them. He'd make it all clear.

"Now remember what we talked about at supper. You are the point of the spear. You have been chosen to carry the holy word to the community. Their salvation is in your hands. What are you going to say?"

"We'll say we love it here?" a man in the back row said, his voice rising questioningly.

"Yes, and we'll say we've found the true way, and they can find it, too."

"I can tell them my bursitis is healed," a fragile lady chimed in.

"And I'll say that all my worries fell away after I learned to trust Emanuel."

"Good, good," Emanuel said. "Really put your hearts into it. Say it like you mean it. Maxine, will you tell them about your widow's mite?"

"If you want me to."

"I do. It's a mighty testimony of your faith. Now, sit up straight. No dozing while I'm talking. I know some of you still feel a little sleepy, but fight it. I want you to look alert."

Everyone shifted, pulling their shoulders back and holding up their heads. Mrs. Entwhistle watched from her seat in the front row. Jacinta sat beside her, still a little silly from her Agua Vita, but at least not giggling.

Mrs. Entwhistle twisted in her seat to see who was arriving. She saw some Busy Bee Diner customers, but no Carol Anne. That was strange. Carol Anne had been the first tip of the sword to be allowed to return to town and go back to her job. Mrs. Entwhistle wondered what had happened to her.

And there was Booger! She was amazed to see him; he never went out in the evening. He was greeting people left and right from his spot beside the tent entrance.

"Evenin', Cora," he called, making his way to her.

"Booger, I didn't expect to see you here."

"Wouldn't 'a missed it. If you need anything— anything a-tall, you just give a shout. I got reinforcements." He patted his overall pocket with a broad wink.

"Oh, now, Booger, there won't be any need of violence," she said.

"We don't rightly know what the need is just yet, do we?" Booger laid his finger beside his nose, arched his eyebrows and nodded. He went back to the door and resumed his greetings. With his white beard and red cheeks, he looked like a disheveled Santa in civvies.

Emanuel's booming bass voice filled the tent. People abruptly stopped talking among themselves as all eyes turned to him.

"Welcome, brothers and sister. Welcome to the first outreach meeting of the Disciples of Holiness. You see before you on the platform the original Disciples, and you see that they are your friends and neighbors, maybe even your relatives. You know them to be good people, fine members of the community. You trust them, and they trust me, so I'm not really a stranger. You know me through them, and you know us through our deeds."

He smiled and raised his arms, his white sleeves billowing. "What was old and worn has become new. Just so will you be renewed when you follow me. We are workers and reapers in His vineyard. Observe the improvements we have made to this old farm in just one week."

His audience obediently looked out the sides of the tent at the freshly-painted barn and the neatly mown grass. They studied the Disciples on the platform, resplendent in their robes.

Emanuel kept talking, but Mrs. Entwhistle's mind wandered. *What pocket did I put that whistle in? I think Booger's carrying that old gun of his in his overall pocket. Everybody knows that Colt has been in his family from the time of the War Between the States. It'll probably blow his hand off if he ever tries to fire it.*

Her attention was jerked back to the present by the sight of Maxine, rising and walking to the front of the platform. Her eyes were glassy and far away, but she seemed composed.

"I'm giving everything I own to Emanuel," she said flatly. "I ask you all to hear his message and open your hearts to what he says."

She sat down again and folded her hands. Mrs. Entwhistle heard the crowd murmur. Most of them had known Maxine forever.

Someone said, "If Maxine's part of the group, maybe there's something to it."

Mrs. Entwhistle saw Dr. Goodlet, looking just like he did in the vet clinic when folks took their sick dogs and cats in for treatment. And Rev. McGill. Several members of his congregation stared in surprise to see their minister in this company. There were Clem and Jane Dearing. Jane waved shyly at one of her friends, then glanced sideways at Clem for approval. She was a little confused, Janie was, and folks had thought it was wise when the Dearings moved to Shady Rest. Clem was known to be the most devoted of husbands, and if he thought this was a good place for Jane, that carried some weight.

One person remained standing in the very back of tent. He had his phone at his side, unobtrusively recording. Occasionally, he'd raise it and take a photograph. Jimmy Jack McNamara was covering the meeting for the *Pantograph*. Rarely did he take on reportorial duties, but if his local beat reporter was here—and he saw her in the front row—then he'd better keep tabs on her. Experience had taught him that.

CHAPTER TEN

Pete and Dex could see the big tent from where they sat in Pete's car. Dex shifted his long legs, stirring the detritus of food wrappers and empty water bottles on the floor. They'd been sitting there for hours. In the rear seat, Axel lay sleeping. He whimpered and paddled his paws as he chased rabbits in his dreams.

"Do you really think that dog is going to hear the whistle if Mrs. E. blows it?" Dex asked. "He's sleeping like a teenager on Saturday morning."

"Well, I guess he would," Pete said doubtfully. "My friend said he comes to life if he thinks he's going to work again. He's highly trained."

Axel snored. Dex eyed the tent.

"I think I'll just go to the tent meeting," he said. "That way I'll be close by if anything happens, and Mrs. E. needs our help."

"I think we should stick to the plan," Pete said. He was a by-the-book lawman, and he hated to deviate from a pre-arranged course of action.

"Look, Emanuel doesn't know me from Adam's house cat. I'll just slip in and sit 'way in the back. Mrs. E. won't see me, and even if she does, she'll know not to react."

Dex carefully opened his car door and slipped out. Axel didn't stir. He closed the door without a sound, flipped a wave at Pete and walked rapidly toward the tent. He had to cross fields in the dark, and the footing was none too even. He stepped in a gopher hole and sprawled on the ground, but he was young and flexible. Picking himself up, he brushed off his clothes and continued. When he entered the tent, he was surprised to find Jimmy Jack, his old editor, standing near the door.

"What are you doing here?" Jimmy Jack whispered.

"I could ask you the same. Are you covering this meeting for the paper?"

"Maybe, if there actually is a story in it. Mostly I'm keeping an eye on Mrs. Entwhistle. I heard she was out here, and it made me nervous to think what she might be up to."

"That's exactly why I'm here," Dex said. The two men grinned at each other. There was a certain fellow-feeling in the necessity and the difficulty of keeping tabs on Mrs. Entwhistle.

"Maxine is here, too." Jimmy Jack indicated the raised platform with a nod of his head. "She looks strange, but she said her piece lucidly enough. She sounded like she'd been thoroughly coached."

They regarded Maxine's glassy gaze. She didn't seem to recognize any of the familiar faces looking back at her.

Emanuel was talking. "I'm going to tell you more about our work, but first, I know y'all must be thirsty. Some of the Disciples are going to pass out water; please have a drink and refresh yourselves before we continue."

Several white-robed figures carrying trays full of paper cups began moving through the tent, murmuring "Bless you!" to each recipient. Jimmy Jack and Dex each snagged a sample.

"Looks okay, smells okay," Jimmy Jack said, raising his cup to his lips.

Dex swatted his arm, spilling the water. "Don't drink it," he said.

Others were not so cautious, and water poured into thirsty throats. There was a hum of conversation as everyone took a break. Jimmy Jack and Dex watched as shoulders relaxed and heads lolled. Folks slumped in their seats when Emanuel began speaking again.

"And now I'm going to ask you to contribute to the work we're doing here. Don't you want to be a part of this great and holy movement? Maybe you can't join us physically at the mission house right now, maybe you have a job, a family, obligations you can't leave, but you can still be a Disciple. Brothers and sisters, I ask you to give from your hearts. Reach deep into your pockets. Be a cheerful giver. The Bible says the Lord loves a cheerful giver."

The patter continued as Disciples moved along the rows with baskets attached to long poles. Men and women dug into their pockets and purses, and bills fluttered.

"Is that all you can give?" Emanuel asked, concern in his voice. "Can't you give just a little bit more? Just an extra dollar or two? Maybe you can make coffee at home instead of buying it. Maybe you can put off trading cars for another year. The electric company won't turn off your power if you're a little late with their bill. They'll understand that you had a better use for your money. The Lord needs your love offering tonight."

Dex rolled his eyes. But people were revisiting their pockets and purses, pulling out more bills. They held up their money and the baskets were passed back to them. Dex noted the absence of coins; no quarters or half-dollars, just bills. He saw tens and twenties and a couple of fifties in the basket when it went by him.

When Emanuel had wrung the last dollar out of the crowd, he motioned for the overflowing baskets to be set before him. Jimmy Jack raised his camera to catch the hungry look on the face of the Disciple in Chief as he eyed the cash. At that moment, Emanuel looked up and saw a phone pointed at him over the heads of the congregation.

"You there! In the back. The one taking pictures. Come forward and let us all see you."

Dex grabbed the phone and walked to the front.

"Yes, sir, I'm the one taking pictures," he said to Emanuel.

Mrs. Entwhistle sat very still in her front-row seat. What in the world was Dex doing here? Where were Pete and the dog?

~*~

Caleb was having trouble. The field adjoining the tent was parked full, and cars lined both sides of the dusty gravel road. He'd deposited Booger close to the door since the old man had trouble walking any distance. Now Caleb crept along looking for someplace to wedge his truck. He finally nosed into the ditch about a quarter mile away and, with a sigh, started walking.

The tent glowed in the dark, and he could hear Emanuel's voice rising and falling as he approached. Caleb was not given to flights of fancy, but he imagined the tent was a space ship swooping to earth to harvest humans and steal their souls. He wished he was home watching TV and drinking beer with his father snoring peacefully in the adjoining bedroom. That's what most of his nights were like.

He entered the tent as Dex strode to the front brandishing a cell phone, and Emanuel met him with widespread arms.

"My brother, you are welcome to take all the photographs you want. You're welcome to record every word that is said here tonight. I have no secrets, nothing to hide. Sit here on the platform with me."

It was not at all what Dex had in mind, but what could he do except take the offered seat at Emanuel's left hand? Mrs. Entwhistle sat just a few feet in front of him. There was a glint of laughter in her eyes before she looked modestly down. He'd never hear the end of this.

From his new vantage point, Dex could see the faces of the crowd. He recognized many of them from his time as a *Pantograph* reporter. He turned to look behind him at the assembled Disciples and saw Jacinta sitting among them. She'd become a Disciple in mid-meeting.

Emanuel was scooping the money from the baskets and stuffing it into a sturdy canvas bag. Dex expected him to hand it off to an usher for safekeeping, but Emanuel slipped the bag inside his robe. He seemed ready to wind things up now that the collection was taken. He stood and raised his arms in benediction. But just as he opened his mouth, a loud voice spoke from the back of the tent.

"Say, I wonder what yer gonna do with that money."

All eyes turned to the speaker. There was a murmur of voices.

"Why, it's Booger."

"That's old Booger."

"What's he think he's doing?"

Booger had his arms crossed over his substantial stomach. His lower lip pouched out and his furry white eyebrows arched to where his hairline once was. His feet were planted wide.

Emanuel stiffened. He moved to neutralize the situation as quickly as possible.

"Come on up here, brother," he invited, sweeping his arm forward.

"Nah, don't care to. Just answer the question: what're you gonna do with all these folks' money?"

"Well, like I said, I'm completely transparent. This love offering will go towards the work of the Disciples of Holiness—"

Booger cut him off. "That means you, don't it? You're the only disciple I see. Th' others are just folks you've roped in someways. Maxine up there, why, I've knowed her for 'bout as long as I've knowed myself. She ain't no disciple, and I don't know what you done to make her think she is."

"Maxine, would you like to stand and answer this gentleman?"

But Maxine was in the grip of a ferocious headache and sat rocking slightly to and fro. She didn't even look up.

"And there's Clem and Janie. Clem, what the hell you thinkin', draggin' Janie out here with this bunch? You know she's better off back at the Shady Rest. And how come you lettin' the preacher drive your car around? He on your insurance? If he has a wreck, you'll git yer policy cancelled for sure."

Clem shook his head as though awakening from an unexpected nap. Jane tugged at his sleeve and said clearly, "I'd like to go home now, honey. Would you just take me on home? I'm so tired."

Booger's searching gaze traveled on. "Reverend McGill, I sure didn't 'spect to see you here. You got a perfickly good church of your own. Is your sermon ready for tomorrow? Tomorrow's Sunday, and your church'll be full. I'll be there, for one. What you gonna tell us?"

Rev. McGill looked around him in surprise. He shook his head, which was beginning to ache, too. Jacinta spoke up beside him.

"Why, Booger, I forgot tomorrow was Sunday, and I don't even have my white shoes polished, nor my good dress ironed for service. Could you give me a ride home?"

But Booger wasn't leaving yet. "Gus Goodlet, you're

just a young fella, and you might be 'scused for bein' gullible. But a lotta people count on you to take care 'o their animals, and you ain't been in your office for a week. There's some sick dogs and cats waitin' for you. You'd best get back there."

Dr. Goodlet's telltale blush spread over his face and down his neck. He nodded once and cast his eyes down.

The mood in the tent shifted, and Caleb tugged his father's arm. "Daddy!" he whispered, "come on, let's get out of here."

Booger shook him off. "You still ain't said what you're gonna do with the cash, preacher. You gonna use it to help the poor? You gonna feed the hungry, or clothe the nekkid?"

Emanuel's eyes darted from side to side, but he saw only unfriendly gazes returned to him. The crowd's warm, dozy good humor was gone. He tried to regain control. "Well, I, uh, I'll be sharing with you my plans for the—"

The clearer-headed among the congregation were standing and coming forward.

"I'll just take back what I gave," one man said, holding out his hand. "I remember exactly how much it was, so I'll thank you to give it back to me."

"I need mine to get the kids' school shoes. I don't know what I was thinking."

Others were rubbing their eyes and passing hands over their foreheads, exchanging confused comments, casting baleful looks at Emanuel.

Mrs. Entwhistle felt the change in the atmosphere, too. It was time to get out of there. She pulled out the dog whistle and clutched it in her hand as she stepped up on the platform and put her hand on Maxine's shoulder.

"Come on, Max. Let's go home now."

Maxine looked up in confusion. "My head, Cora, it hurts."

But Emanuel wasn't giving up. "Now hold on, everybody just sit back down. Y'all gave that money of your own free will. It belongs to the Disciples of Holiness now, and you can't just take it back."

"Reckon they can, preacher," Booger said. "Reckon they're gonna do just that, even if they have to strip that nightgown off'n you to get it."

He walked forward and stood directly in front of Emanuel. Thrusting one hand in his overall pocket, he eased out the old Colt just enough to be visible. Emanuel's eyes widened.

Jacinta's shriek raised the tent roof. "Gun! Gun!"

She threw herself on the floor directly behind Emanuel so that he tripped over her when he stepped back. He airplaned his arms trying to regain his balance, his hand making contact with Mrs. Entwhistle's shoulder. Grabbing her, he pulled her close and put his arm around her neck. Later, she'd say she didn't know how she did it, but somehow she raised the dog whistle to her lips. She managed one strong blow before he knocked it from her mouth.

Dex, Caleb and Booger approached Emanuel warily. Booger was holding his old gun, but he pointed it at the ground.

"Stay back, or I'll snap her neck," Emanuel snarled. "Everybody stay back. She's coming with me and don't try to stop me, or you'll be going to a funeral."

He tightened his hold on Mrs. Entwhistle's neck. She pawed at his arm, but it was like a steel band constricting her airway. A rolling cloud of blackness licked at the corners of her vision.

"Don't you pass out now, Cora Entwhistle!" *Was that Floyd's voice?* "Stand up straight and lean back into him." She did, relieving the worst of the pressure on her neck.

Emanuel backed out of the tent slowly, holding Mrs. Entwhistle in front of him. He was heading toward Clem's car. She knew if he got her into that car, she was a goner. He'd wait until he was far enough away, and then who knows what he'd do? Push her out of a speeding vehicle? Finish the job of strangling her? It wouldn't be pretty, she was sure of that.

Suddenly, she was on the ground. A snarling whirlwind ripped off Emanuel's robe and sank its fangs into his thigh. Agonized screams and frantic thrashing didn't deter the animal; it held on like it was never going to let go. Mrs. Entwhistle recoiled from a solid kick in the ribs as Emanuel fell under the ferocity of his attacker.

How pretty, all those green butterflies fluttering, fluttering. Oh, wait, its money. Mrs. Entwhistle closed her eyes and went somewhere else for a few minutes. When she came to herself again, it was to see the concerned face of Dex Shofield in very close proximity to her own.

"Mrs. E! Mrs. E! Can you hear me?"

"No need to shout."

"Are you okay? Can you move your legs? There's a pool of something red under you. Is it blood?"

Mrs. Entwhistle took inventory: yes, she could move

her arms and legs and her mind seemed to be working again. She squinted down at the red pool soaking into the ground beneath her and shook her head.

"No, Dex. It's Hawaiian punch. I was wearing it."

CHAPTER ELEVEN

"Well, I just feel like a pure fool," Maxine said.

She was sitting on Mrs. Entwhistle's porch swing, holding Martin in her lap. The big cat was purring and arching his back under her stroking hand. Roger sat a respectful distance away and watched from the corner of his eye. He'd learned not to look directly at Martin, who tended to regard it as a challenge.

Mrs. Entwhistle was stringing beans, delivered fresh from Booger's garden earlier that day. He'd brought them himself, then stood twisting his straw hat, waiting for her to invite him to sit.

"I'm afraid this isn't a good time, Booger," Mrs. Entwhistle said firmly. "I sure do thank you, not only for the beans, but for what you did at the tent meeting. If you hadn't challenged Emanuel about the collection money, there's no telling what else he might have gotten away with."

"Welcome," Booger mumbled, looking at the horizon. He could be shy sometimes.

"I'm right busy this morning. Maxine's staying with me for a few days until she gets to feeling herself again. Again, thank you kindly." She made her voice sound final, but Booger wasn't getting it.

"Maybe you'd like to go to the Busy Bee for a cuppa coffee one mornin' after Maxine goes home," he ventured. "Or tea, you can have tea if you'd druther."

Mrs. Entwhistle thought of the tidal wave of gossip that would wash over the town at such an appearance. It wouldn't do. She'd pussy-footed around Booger long enough. He was completely recovered from his heart attack, and she needn't worry about bringing on another one. The last thing she wanted to do was hurt his feelings, but it was kinder, in the long run, to speak plainly.

"Booger, I think you're looking for romance and that's fine, but I'm just not interested."

She had to press her lips together to keep from smiling at the thought of Booger and romance in the same sentence. She didn't want him to think she was laughing at him.

"But doncha get lonesome sometimes?" Booger asked. "Floyd's been gone a long time."

"Yes, and I still miss him every day, but I'm not grieving. I've adjusted to being alone, and now I just want a peaceful life, that's all."

"Pardon my sayin' so, but seein' the crazy things that are always happenin' to you, it don't look peaceful to me."

"It does seem I have more misadventures than most, but I don't go looking for trouble. And I certainly don't need the kind of trouble I'd get if I took up with an old codger—" She managed to stop herself from finishing the sentence, "like you."

But Booger heard the words she didn't speak.

"I won't bother you no more, then," he said with dignity.

"I'm sorry, Booger, but I think it's better to be honest."

Booger dipped his chin. "I'd best be gettin' home. Enjoy them beans." He walked to his old truck where Caleb waited.

Maxine shook her head when Mrs. Entwhistle

relayed the conversation to her later. "Now you've hurt his feelings, and you know how Booger can pout. You'll have to apologize, and then he'll get his hopes up again."

"Booger's a tough old boot. He'll get over it," Mrs. Entwhistle said callously. Really, she couldn't worry about everybody, and her focus right now was on Maxine.

"How are you feeling today, Max? Is your headache gone?"

"Yes, finally. Whatever was in that water sent me to la-la land, and re-entry hurt."

"It wasn't only you; everyone had withdrawal headaches. It'll be interesting to see what the lab test shows on that sample of water the sheriff sent off for testing. Poor Dr. Goodlet missed two more days of work sick in bed, and Jacinta says her head still hurts, but I think she's just trying to get attention. Do you know, she's telling everyone she sounded the alarm that led to Emanuel's capture?"

"She did scream GUN!" Maxine laughed. "That even got through my brain fog. And then when I saw Emanuel grab you..." The laughter died and Maxine's eyes welled with tears. "It was all my fault. You could have been hurt or even killed because I was so stupid."

"You're not stupid, Max, now don't you say that. You would never have fallen for Emanuel's scam if you hadn't been drugged. That tea party y'all had, I'd bet my Social Security check that when you went to answer the phone, he slipped something into your cup. It hit you hard, and you were so out of it that it was easy for him to load you in the car and take you away."

"But you always tell me not to let strangers in my house. I wish I'd listened."

"Never mind, Max. It's over now. The important thing is, you're home and safe."

"Does your rib hurt, Cora?"

"Well, it does, some, when I bend down or reach for something, but it's getting better every day. I don't think Emanuel really meant to kick me; his feet just flew out from under him when Axel took him down, and I was in the way. Say, wasn't that dog something? Pete said he'd been sound asleep in the back seat of the car, but he leaped out the window in a flash when he heard the whistle. Pete had to run after him as fast as he could, but by the time he caught up, Axel had Emanuel on the ground."

"I'm going to get that dog a nice piece of steak,"

Maxine said.

They were interrupted by a car pulling into the driveway.

"Oh, there's Pete now."

It was not only Pete; Axel was riding shotgun in the passenger seat. He hopped stiffly down when Pete opened the door. It was hard to believe the arthritic canine before them was the same snarling beast who'd subdued a con man.

"Just checking on my two favorite ladies," Pete said.

"We're fine, Pete, thanks to you and Axel. Say, why hasn't he gone back to his owner?"

"My friend has been assigned another K-9 partner, and it's simpler not to have a working dog and a retired dog in the same house."

"Oh, no. What will become of poor Axel?"

"Well, I guess I've got me a dog," Pete said, grinning sheepishly. "The boys are thrilled."

"Is he good with them? He hasn't been used to children."

"Turns out he loves kids, even tolerates Corrie yanking on his ears."

"Pete, what happened to Emanuel?" Maxine asked. "Last I heard, Sheriff Martinez was holding him in our little jail."

"The sheriff was happy to turn him over to the Feds and let them have the expense of incarcerating and eventually trying him. He's bound to get life without parole with all those counts of kidnapping against him."

"Did people get their offerings back?"

"In a way. They decided to donate the money to the food pantry, most of it, anyway. I suspect a few people might have pocketed some of the bills that were blowing around on the ground that night."

Whomp.

The *Pantograph* hit the front steps, tossed by a boy on a bike. Pete bent over to retrieve it, shook the paper out of its plastic wrapper and opened it. The front page stories for the last several days had been detailed accounts of the Disciples debacle. Mrs. Entwhistle wondered how many more stories Jimmy Jack could wring out of it. Today's banner headline read, HERO DOG SAVES LOCALS. There was an old photograph of Axel, taken in his glory days as a police dog.

"My, he does look handsome, doesn't he?" Maxine

said admiringly. She glanced down. "In the paper, that is."

The real-life Axel was snoring most unhandsomely, stretched out on his side with a little drool pool beneath his muzzle. He was deeply asleep, oblivious of Roger and Martin. The big tomcat chose that moment to remind Maxine it was his dinner time. He rose to his feet, stretched and issued an earsplitting "MEOW."

Axel was up in an instant, hackles raised. He let loose a volley of thunderous barks, making everyone jump a foot. Martin's ears flattened, his back arched and his tail doubled in size. Despite the loudest hiss he could manage, he seemed to realize he was seriously punching above his weight. He shrank back into Maxine's lap, pretending a profound interest in the bird feeder.

Roger smiled.

Floyd's Secret

Floyd had been dead for years before Mrs. Entwhistle found the box. Not that she was looking for it. She'd finally been clearing out his tool shed, a task that really should have fallen to their son, Tommy. After Floyd's passing, she'd invited Tommy and Diane to take whatever they wanted of Floyd's possessions, which were mostly tools.

"Just leave me the basics, a good hammer, pliers, screwdrivers, that kind of thing. I sure don't need a vise, or car jacks, or a 40-foot extension ladder."

The kids took her at her word. They cleaned out most of Floyd's tools, and he'd had a lot of them. When they were finished, Mrs. Entwhistle shut and locked the shed door. Although the space was nearly empty, it was still so evocative of Floyd's presence that she couldn't bear to enter.

Now she contemplated the little building as she

stood at the kitchen window drinking her morning tea. A wave of ambition crested over her. Today was the day. Today she'd clear out the remaining detritus from Floyd's tool shed. She'd be a grown-up and deal with it.

She'd remember to check for a hornets' nest above the door, one of their favorite haunts, before she opened it. She would not scream if mice scurried from the wood stacked in the corner. She'd shed no tears over the worn-out office chair that Floyd pulled up to sit at his workbench. It still bore the imprint of his posterior, but she'd ignore that. She'd get the job done once and for all.

Wrapping her head in a bandana against spiders and carrying her cleaning supplies in a bucket, Mrs. Entwhistle marched into the back yard. The determined set of her chin signaled that whatever she was after didn't stand a chance. Two hours later, the trash can was full and the shelves and hooks were empty.

"Hmmm. Might make a nice playhouse for Tommy's girls," she mused aloud, surveying the empty space. "We could bring down the play kitchen and the doll's bed from the attic."

Then she remembered that Tommy's girls were twelve and fourteen. They'd heap scorn on such an idea, but Dex's little one might enjoy a play house in a few years.

"Or maybe I could make one of those she-sheds. Put down a pretty rug, get some wicker furniture..." She looked about doubtfully. What would be the point, really? Her house was full of places to sit without her trekking out to a shed in the back yard.

Oh well, she could figure out what to do with the building later. Meanwhile, she'd give it a good sweeping.

She plied her broom, brushing down cobwebs and raising a storm of dust on the floor. Pursuing a web in a dark corner of the rafters, she encountered resistance. Something solid was up there. She couldn't see what it was and the temptation to ignore it was strong, but she had resolved to do the job thoroughly. She fetched her three-step ladder and a flashlight. Climbing up, she shone the light timidly, ready to jump, hoping nothing would fly at her from a disturbed nest. No, it was metal, whatever it was. She poked at it. It didn't seem heavy. She lifted it from its spidery nest and climbed down carefully.

It was a small, fireproof, metal box, the kind you keep important papers in, with a combination lock securing the lid. Mrs. Entwhistle turned the box over to see, knowing Floyd, if the combination was taped to the bottom. Nope. She turned the dial to Floyd's birthday. Nothing. Tried her birthday, their wedding date, the kids' birthdays. Nothing. Frustrated, she shook it, trying to guess what might be inside. That had never worked with Christmas packages, and it didn't work now, either.

Carrying the box outside into the sunshine, she eased herself down on the doorstep. Floyd wasn't very security-minded, and she was surprised he'd not used one of the easy-to-remember dates in their family's life. Idly, she turned the dial: one, two, three, four, five.

Click.

The lock opened. Shaking her head and smiling, she raised the lid.

Inside was the deed to the house—she'd searched high and low for that deed!—the title to the Buick now covered with a tarp and permanently asleep in the garage, a copy of their mutual will, and a small, white, cardboard box.

She opened the box.

On a nest of fluffy cotton lay a large, unset red stone. It caught the morning sun and reflected a painful flash of light directly into her eyes. Mrs. Entwhistle blinked and covered the stone with her hand.

What in the world? Why had Floyd packed away a gaudy piece of glass so carefully? Was he planning to surprise her? She glanced down at her left hand, where she still wore her wedding and engagement rings. Floyd had given her his mother's diamond ring when he proposed, a dim old solitaire set in rose gold. She'd loved it ever since he'd put it on her finger and had seldom taken it off. Even if this red hunk had been set in a ring, she'd never wear such a thing.

Mrs. Entwhistle couldn't be babying some fancy glass ring when she needed to weed the garden or scrub the porch swing, and Floyd knew that. He certainly wouldn't have meant to wear it himself. His work at the Bell Bomber plant precluded jewelry of any kind. Mrs. Entwhistle had secretly breathed a sigh of relief when he came home at the end of his shifts with ten intact fingers. Some of his co-workers sported stubs.

So why would Floyd have gotten a big fake ruby? *Where did he get it? What was he intending to do with it? Why had he hidden it and never mentioned it?*

In a setting, it would be what her high-school friends used to call a knuckle-duster. She smiled at the thought of swishing into the Busy Bee Diner flashing that big red honker and asking Herve' for an order of blueberry pancakes.

Maybe it was a joke of some kind. That seemed doubtful, though; Floyd wasn't a big joker. But if it had been real, it would have cost a packet, and Floyd didn't have a packet. Did he? He'd handled their finances, dutifully depositing his paycheck in the bank every week, taking out a little cash for himself and handing her the household money. Of course, she knew she could get whatever she wanted or needed, but they were both frugal.

That's why it had been such a joy to share her Publisher's Clearing House winnings. She'd given away almost all the money, in fact. When Floyd's pension fund went belly-up and she needed more income, she'd found a job as a local beat reporter at the *Pantograph,* the town's newspaper. It turned out to be one of the most rewarding ventures of her life. Not only had it kept her mind ticking along briskly, she'd met Dex Shofield, a young intern, and their shared adventures had forged a strong friendship. He was one of her favorite people in all the world. In addition, she privately believed she'd saved the editor, Jimmy Jack McNamara, from his own indolence, ignorance and indecision. Not that she ever would have said so.

Pulling her thoughts back to the present, Mrs.

Entwhistle held the red stone up to the light again and was rewarded by another painful flash in the eyes. She dropped it back into its box, put the lid on and slipped it into her pocket.

"I need to talk this over with Maxine," she said to Roger, who lay on the grass waiting patiently for her to return them both to the house where they belonged. She carried him inside and plopped him on his favorite sofa cushion. No point in bothering Max with a phone call to say she was coming over. She just went.

"Hi, Cora, I'm canning peaches," Maxine called from the kitchen when Mrs. Entwhistle entered her house without knocking.

Mrs. Entwhistle got a paring knife from the block beside the stove, settled into a chair and grabbed some fruit from the wooden basket on the floor. She peeled expertly while she told Maxine about what she'd found in the shed.

"Did you bring it?" Maxine asked, wiping her hands on her apron. "Let's see."

Mrs. Entwhistle reached in her pocket, pulled out the white box and handed it to Maxine. Maxine's eyes widened when she saw the contents.

"Who? What? Who?" she sputtered.

"You look and sound like an owl," Mrs. Entwhistle said mildly. "It's as big a mystery to me as to you. Why Floyd would get such a gaudy old thing and then hide it... I wonder if I'll ever know. What d'you think it is?"

Maxine had some nice pieces of jewelry. Her husband had simplified the gift-giving process by presenting Max with a ring, bracelet, necklace, or earrings for every occasion. At first, it was just costume jewelry, but as he and Maxine grew more solvent, he invested in real gemstones. Maxine had gotten interested. She'd read a few books on how to recognize and evaluate gems, and had even gotten a jeweler's loupe. Now she abandoned the peaches and went to get her loupe.

"Okay, let's have a look," she said. She held the lens close to her eye, bringing the stone up close. "Hmmm. Bright red color. No orange peel."

"What does that mean?"

"No mold marks," Maxine muttered, ignoring her.

She might as well have been speaking Urdu for all Mrs. Entwhistle knew.

Maxine continued her perusal, twisting the stone in her hand. "The fact that there are tiny, tiny flaws is good," she said. "Real stones have them, fakes don't.

The facets are sharp and clear, too."

She lowered the loupe and took up her paring knife, scratching it against the stone's surface. "No mark."

She rubbed it hard against the window over the sink. "No color rubs off. Did you know a natural ruby is actually the red version of a sapphire? It becomes red when high amounts of chromium are present during the stone's formation. Which takes millions of years."

Mrs. Entwhistle shrugged. Maxine looked her in the eye and repeated, "*Millions. Of. Years.* Think about it."

"Well, swanee, you don't have to be so dramatic," Mrs. Entwhistle said. "This one's just red glass, isn't it? Something Floyd picked up for some crazy reason?"

"I don't think its glass," Maxine said solemnly. "I think it might be a real ruby. I'm no expert, but you need one. If it's a real ruby, you've got to have it insured. It could be worth a lot."

"My stars," said Mrs. Entwhistle. "What in the world was Floyd thinking?"

That was a question she turned over and over in her mind that night as she lay in bed waiting for sleep.

Where would Floyd have gotten the money to pay for a real ruby? What was he planning to do with it? He was such a practical man. If he'd had extra funds, he'd have been much more likely to buy her a new freezer or something. Did he mean the ruby to be an investment? It would be hard to liquidate in an emergency. Didn't sound like something Floyd would do at all. She repressed a renegade thought that perhaps Floyd meant to give it to someone else. Not Floyd. Surely not.

Mrs. Entwhistle dreamed about him that night. He looked the way he had as a young man, strong and capable. When he reached out his hand to her, she eagerly reached back—until she saw the enormous blood-red ruby on his finger. She recoiled, and Floyd looked hurt.

"I got it for you," he said.

"But why? Why did you think I'd want it?"

The ruby began to ooze blood. It dripped down Floyd's outstretched hand and made a puddle on the ground. He seemed not to notice, not even after she tried to scream. Nothing came out but a rusty squeak, but it woke her. She sat up in bed, her heart galloping.

"Floyd, what did you do?" she said aloud.

Roger slept on. Now that he was almost completely deaf, not much disturbed him. Thunder, which used to strike terror into his heart, rumbled unnoticed. Even when she turned on the light and got out of bed, he didn't move.

There'd be no more sleeping for her, and she resigned herself to starting the day at four a.m. Wrapped in her chenille robe, she took her cup of tea to the porch swing. The sky was still velvety black but there was a noticeable lightening in the east. She rocked, sipped and tried to put her thoughts in logical order.

Floyd had somehow come by a red stone. It might or might not be a real ruby. The first thing to do was get it evaluated by an expert. There was no such person in her small town, so that meant a trip to the city. She knew she couldn't ride her scooter in that kind of traffic, so she'd have to ask Maxine to drive her. She was sure that would be fine with Max; there'd be no keeping her away from a mystery like this.

So I'll have to find an expert, but thank goodness there's the Internet for that. What did we used to do, pre-Internet? How did we ever find anything? I don't know who to trust, that's the trouble. The older I get, the more I feel like the world is full of sharks out to cheat me. I miss the days when I believed I could trust people. Is it me, or has society really changed? Maybe all old people reach the same conclusion as their ability to cope fades.

At the idea of her coping abilities declining, she sat up straight and tightened her jaw. She wasn't senile yet. She still had all her marbles and she'd use 'em. Floyd may have had the best intentions, but he'd certainly complicated her life by leaving behind this mysterious gem. That happened sometimes. Good intentions went sideways and people just had to cope. If there was one thing she could do, it was cope. It was just a matter of getting organized. She went to her laptop.

She found the names and contact information of two companies that claimed to appraise gems. Raising her phone, she snapped a picture of the red stone and attached it to a brief message to each of them. Characteristically, she didn't dwell on the thought of what she might do with the money if the stone was valuable. One step at a time.

Roger came down the stairs cautiously. She watched, afraid he'd miss a step and take a tumble. That had happened before. She met him halfway, scooped him up and carried him into the kitchen.

"How about bacon and eggs, Rog? I've been up for hours and I could eat!"

Roger allowed that he could, too.

~*~

The minute she saw him, Mrs. Entwhistle thought the man behind the counter looked sneaky. Tall, tailored, and wearing a pair of tortoise-shell glasses, he was just a shade too good to be true, like the Hollywood version of a gem expert. That impression was strengthened when he smiled, revealing double rows of extremely white teeth.

"May I help you ladies?" he asked with a tiny bow in their direction.

Mrs. Entwhistle noticed he snuck a glimpse of himself in the mirror that hung opposite. Vain people really shouldn't place mirrors anywhere in their own vicinity, she thought. The temptation's just too great.

Maxine took over. "Yes, thank you. I'm Maxine, and this is Cora Entwhistle. She e-mailed you about the red stone?"

"Ah, yes. The large red stone," the man said, his voice conveying disdain of the stone and the sender. "Do you have it with you?"

Mrs. Entwhistle stepped forward. "I do."

"I can take a look at it, if you'd like."

"That's why I'm here." She plunked down the box. "I presume you are Mr. Lacey of Lacey's Fine Gems?"

"I am, indeed. Now, if I may."

He drew the white box toward himself and Mrs. Entwhistle had to stop her hand from grabbing it back. She may not have cared much for the stone, but it had been Floyd's. This guy made her spine tingle and not in a good way.

She watched as he employed a much more serious-looking loupe than Maxine's. He held the red stone up to his eye, and his whole demeanor changed. The superior attitude vanished. He bent forward with an audible intake of breath.

"I, uh, I need to take this stone into my workroom where I have more magnification," he said, turning toward the back of the store.

"I'll go with you," Mrs. Entwhistle said firmly. This man wasn't walking off with Floyd's stone. No telling what he might substitute for it when out of sight. She hated to think that way, but she did.

She kept her eyes peeled as Lacey hurried to a work table where another man was seated.

"Look at this, Hank."

Something in Lacey's voice caused the other man to

stop what he was doing and raise an interested face. "What you got there?"

"I'm not sure, but if it's what I think it might be...."

Lacey placed the red stone on the table. It caught the overhead fluorescent light and sent back a stab of color. Mrs. Entwhistle stepped closer, crowding between the two men in order to keep the stone in sight as Hank examined it.

It took a while. Hank used a number of different instruments. He measured with calipers, jotting notes of the results. He muttered terms like *refractive index* and *birefringence* and *fluorescence.* He shook his head; he bit his lip; he whispered to himself; he ran both hands through his hair, making it stand on end, and said, "Holy guacamole!"

Finally, Hank looked up and addressed Mrs. Entwhistle. "Are you the owner of this stone?"

"Well, my late husband was; I only recently found it. Yes, I own it, I guess."

"Madam, I need to do more testing, and it will take some time. Can you leave the stone with me?"

"What's your first impression? Is it valuable?"

Hank's tone was condescending. "I see you are unfamiliar with gemstones. I'm not prepared to give a dollar figure right now, but my initial assessment is that this stone may have some value. It may be Burmese."

"Is that good?"

Hank and Lacey glanced at each other and then back at her. Something in their eyes rang alarm bells in Mrs. Entwhistle's head. She'd learned to heed those bells.

"I won't leave it, thank you," she said, picking it up and putting it back in the box. She didn't miss the way Hank's hand reached out involuntarily to stop her.

"Of course, if that is what madam wishes," Lacey said, his voice dripping disapproval. "Only madam should know that unless this stone is insured—is it?"

She shook her head.

"Then it is most unwise to carry it around."

"I'll be very careful. Thank you for your time. What do I owe you?" Mrs. Entwhistle asked. She may not have liked these two, but she always paid her way.

"We will waive our customary appraisal fee," Lacey said with a smile that made Mrs. Entwhistle think about sharks. "Of course, we hope you will return and allow us to examine the stone more thoroughly, and perhaps consider selling it to us once a value has been established. You must be cautious in your dealings with gemstone experts. I'm sorry to say there is fraud in the trade."

Yeah, and I'll bet you know all about that, Mrs. Entwhistle thought. She clutched the little white box with both hands as she and Maxine left the store.

"On to the next guy," Maxine said cheerfully. "I don't know about you, but I didn't care much for Mr. Lacey. What was the fellow in the back like?"

"Didn't like him, either," Mrs. Entwhistle said. "They both gave me the heebie-jeebies. I hope the next place will be better."

And it was. For one thing, the appraiser was a woman of Asian descent. She was young and beautiful, radiating warmth and welcome. Mrs. Entwhistle was instantly captivated as she met Kyi Kra.

"Aren't you young to be in this line of work, Miss Kra?" she asked.

"Please, call me Kiki. In Burmese, there are no surnames. Every person gets a unique name, and every name has meaning. Even though I was born in this country, my father went back to the old ways to name me Kyi Kra, which means joyous water lily. I love my Burmese name, but it's easier for my American friends to say Kiki."

Kiki beamed at Mrs. Entwhistle, who smiled back and nodded.

"To answer your question, I am young, yes, but I'm certified by the Gemological Institute of America. I work with my father, who is also certified. Would you feel more comfortable with him?"

"No, Kiki, I feel perfectly comfortable with you. I've brought something to show you."

Again, she watched as the gemologist turned her attention to the stone. Kiki looked for a long time, then she lowered her loupe and met Mrs. Entwhistle's eyes.

"What you have here is very special and, I believe, very valuable," Kiki said. "I need to run some tests and have my father confirm my findings. It will take a week. Will you leave the stone with me? I know it's scary; we've just met."

Mrs. Entwhistle and Maxine exchanged glances; Maxine nodded slightly. Mrs. Entwhistle decided. "Why, Kiki, I'm not a bit scared to leave the stone with you."

There was paperwork, of course, and Kiki's's father, Aung Cho, came from the back room to meet them. It all was accomplished with cordiality and dispatch, and soon they found themselves back on the sidewalk. Mrs. Entwhistle had a receipt in her purse and a funny feeling in her stomach.

"Maybe I'm hungry," she said. "I feel peculiar."

"Let's get a cup of tea. Look, here's a little place, and it's got outside tables." Maxine purely loved to eat outdoors. She was always downcast when winter weather confined her to her kitchen table.

The ladies ordered a pot of English Breakfast tea and two scones, but Mrs. Entwhistle found she wasn't hungry, after all. She picked her scone apart without tasting a bite. It was unlike her; normally, she had a good appetite, and she never wasted food.

"Cora, are you okay?"

"Oh, yes, I'm fine. It's just that I feel so strange about that stone." She couldn't quite call it a ruby; not yet. "It's made me think I didn't know Floyd at all."

"Why, of course, you knew him," Maxine said. "You were married to him for half a century."

"Yes, but do we ever really know another human being? I would have said the least likely person in the world to have a hidden treasure would be Floyd Entwhistle. Yet he did, and I wonder if I'll ever know why. It's so frustrating not to be able to ask him."

They sat silently pondering the fathomless abyss between the living and the dead. Maxine got a gleam in her eye.

"Do you remember that fortune teller we went to a couple of times, Madame Esmeralda?" she asked. "The one who came to the county fair?"

"It wasn't always the same woman," Mrs. Entwhistle said. "Seemed to be whoever they could get to wear that turban."

Maxine brushed aside such nit-picking. "She told me some stuff, remember, about my old dog, Jingo. And she knew you were going shopping for a car."

"She said you'd get a new dog, but you got a cat instead."

"Still, I did get a pet. And she said you shouldn't buy a car, and you didn't. How did she know?"

Mrs. Entwhistle managed not to say even a blind hog finds an acorn now and then. She didn't want to be unkind. If Maxine liked to believe in communication with the spirit world, after all, who did it hurt? Still, she was glad the county fair was not in season, and

Maxine couldn't drag her to the current Madame Esmeralda for whatever mumbo-jumbo was on offer. But she'd reckoned too soon.

"I bet we could find a psychic right here in the city," Maxine said. "Wouldn't you like to know where Floyd got that ruby, and what he had in mind?"

"You know I don't believe in psychics and all that mess."

"I know, but it'd be fun," Maxine said, and bent her head over her phone, poking laboriously with one finger in the Search bar. "Nothing ventured, nothing gained...Yes! Here's one." She pulled up a photograph of a woman with her face half-hidden by veils.

They were interrupted by the waitress bringing their food. Maxine squinted at the waitress' name tag. "Billie, do you know anything about this psychic?" she asked, holding out her phone.

Billie glanced at the picture tiredly. Everything about Billie looked weary: her hair drooped, her face drooped, and her ankles drooped over her thick white shoes. But when she saw the face in Maxine's phone, she perked up.

"Why, that's Jasmina," she said. "My neighbor went to her last year when she was pregnant. Jasmina told her the baby would be a boy, would look like his daddy, and would learn to walk before he was one."

Mrs. Entwhistle stifled a snort. Pretty safe predictions all around. Jasmina had a one in two chance of being right about the gender, and the proud parents would paper over any other discrepancies.

"And did it come true?" Maxine breathed.

"Well, it was a girl, but she did look like her father. That was too bad, actually. But she walked real early."

Maxine nodded eagerly. "Where is this Jasmina located?"

"Not too far from here. She's got a store-front right by the butcher shop on Delancey Street."

"Max, I don't think...."

"Oh, come on, Cora, let's just do it. Maybe you'll hear something helpful, and if you don't, well, no harm, no fool."

It was such an engagingly mangled idiom that Mrs. Entwhistle had to acquiesce.

~*~

It took them half an hour to find it. Delancey turned out to be a twisting street that changed its name in mid-block, but finally Mrs. Entwhistle spotted a shop window bearing a large hand-painted eye.

"Stop! There it is," she said. "That must be it."

After a search for a parking place Maxine was able to deposit her car, and they walked to the store front. Under the large eye were the words, "Jasmina, Clairvoyant for the Ages. Your past, present and future in a nutshell."

"I'll bet the nut part is right, anyway," Mrs. Entwhistle said grumpily. "Come on, Max, let's get this over with."

Jasmina's domain looked just about the way Mrs. Entwhistle expected it to: A dusty velvet settee piled with pillows, beaded curtains at the window, and a business-like cash box perched on the counter. The woman behind the counter looked familiar now that they saw her unveiled.

"Why, you're Esmeralda the Magnificent," Maxine said. She was better at remembering faces and names than Mrs. Entwhistle was.

"I'm only Esmeralda when I'm working the fairs, honey. Here at home, I'm Jasmina," the woman explained.

"You told our fortunes a few years back," Maxine said. "And you were pretty close to right, too."

Jasmina looked them over carefully. Her eyes widened, and she nodded decisively when she inspected Mrs. Entwhistle.

"I remember you," she said, ignoring Maxine. "You were going to buy a car and I told you not to. Did you take my advice?"

"I didn't buy a car, but I don't think it was because of your advice. I really don't believe in psychic stuff. No offense."

"Yes, I remember you said that then, too, and yet here you are again. What can I do for you?"

Maxine launched into a detailed explanation about the mysterious stone. Jasmina's black eyes never left Mrs. Entwhistle, who squirmed under such close scrutiny.

"So we thought, well, *I* thought maybe you could tell us something about the stone," Maxine finished.

"I wish you'd brought it," Jasmina said. "I need to touch something. I guess you'll have to do."

Jasmina grasped Mrs. Entwhistle's hand and closed her eyes. She inhaled and exhaled in long, noisy aspirations. Mrs. Entwhistle couldn't suppress an eye roll, causing Maxine to shake her head reproachfully. Finally, Jasmina spoke, her eyes still closed.

"I see a young man. He is in a big city in a foreign land. All around him is noise. He does not speak the language. There is a beautiful girl. She and the young man are talking. Their heads are close together. She opens her hand, and a red stone in her palm catches the sun. The young man shields his eyes. He takes the stone."

Mrs. Entwhistle found she was holding her breath. She waited, but Jasmina seemed to be done talking.

"What happened next?" Mrs. Entwhistle asked in a voice not quite her own.

"I don't know," Jasmina said tersely. "That's all I got."

The seer didn't look well. Her skin was pale and clammy. Sweat beaded her upper lip.

"Who were they, the young man and the beautiful girl?" Maxine asked.

"I don't know," Jasmina said. "I told you what I saw, and that's all I know."

"Huh. What do I owe you?" Mrs. Entwhistle said, taking out her wallet resignedly.

"Nothing. No charge," Jasmina said, blotting her face with a tissue. "Free today. Please go now."

"Couldn't you try again? Maybe you could tell us a little more," Maxine pleaded, but Jasmina shook her head.

Mrs. Entwhistle pulled Maxine toward the door, and they were almost outside when Jasmina said, "Wait." They turned back to her.

She looked directly at Mrs. Entwhistle. "I don't actually see things. You know that."

Mrs. Entwhistle nodded. Maxine looked crestfallen.

"But that time before and again today...with you, I do. I see things. And I don't like the way it makes me feel. Don't ever come back."

Without another word, Jasmina disappeared into the back room, shutting the door firmly behind her. Maxine and Mrs. Entwhistle didn't speak until they were back in the car.

"What do you think?" Maxine asked quietly. Her usual enthusiasm was muted by the strange encounter.

"Oh, Max, it's just an act. You heard her say she doesn't really see things."

"Yes, but she said with you, she does. Do you think Floyd was the young man? And who could the beautiful girl have been? I bet it was you," Maxine said loyally.

"I think I'd remember giving Floyd a ruby. Nope, it was just an act. That's what she does to make money."

"She didn't take any money from you," Maxine pointed out.

Mrs. Entwhistle had no answer for that.

She tried to forget it. She didn't believe in contact with the spirit world, and Jasmina/Esmeralda had admitted she was a fake. Why give credence to her strange scenario of a young man, a beautiful girl and a red stone? Jasmina'd probably seen something like that on television and trotted it out for the gullible. Mrs. Entwhistle resolved to put the whole thing out of her mind.

The week until the appraisal would be ready seemed to stretch on and on. Mrs. Entwhistle weeded the garden, washed and ironed the curtains in the guest room, gave Roger a bath, waxed her scooter and took homemade cookies to the fire station. Finally, exactly a week since the red stone had been surrendered to Kiki and her father, Maxine drove them back to the jeweler's shop. They'd been asked to arrive before the shop opened so they could hear the appraisal without interruptions. Promptly at nine a.m., Mrs. Entwhistle rapped softly on the shop's glass door.

Kiki answered herself, greeting them like old friends as she ushered them through the showroom and into the workroom in the back where her father waited.

"Thank you for giving us the opportunity to evaluate your ruby," Aung Cho said formally. "I consider myself privileged to have examined such a stone even once in my career."

"Then it's not glass?" Mrs. Entwhistle asked.

"No, indeed, my dear lady. It is not glass. It is a ruby of great value." He handed Mrs. Entwhistle a stiff white sheet of paper headed "Authentication."

> **"Rare Burmese two-carat ruby, emerald cut, pure red. Eye clean, heat only. Typical of stones from the Mogok Stone Tract, this is a true pigeon's blood ruby with a distinctive fluorescence."**

There was a lot more, but Mrs. Entwhistle stopped reading when she saw the estimated value.

"How do you wish to proceed? Do you want the gem set? Shall we assist you in finding a buyer?" Aung Cho asked hopefully. "For the honor of placing such a gem, I would ask only half my usual commission."

Mrs. Entwhistle couldn't think what to do. She looked to Maxine for help.

"I don't think she's quite ready to decide about that yet," Maxine said. "Thank you for your services and for being so nice. We sure appreciate it, hear?"

~*~

Later, Mrs. Entwhistle couldn't remember leaving the shop. Somehow, she and Maxine had gotten out the door and back into the car. Maxine hadn't suggested a stop at the outdoor cafe this time. Neither of them spoke as they drove home.

When they were settled in Mrs. Entwhistle's kitchen with mugs of tea, Maxine stretched her hand across the table and asked, "Cora? Are you all right?"

"I'm not sure."

"It was good news, wasn't it? The ruby is worth a lot of money."

"Yes. It seems to be."

Five hundred thousand dollars. That's what Kiki and

her father said, what they certified with their signatures, putting their professional reputations on the line.

"That's what you'd could expect selling it privately. At auction, it might well fetch a higher price," Aung Cho had said, while Kiki beamed with pride as if she'd found the ruby herself.

Auction? How would she even go about setting up such a thing? Who could she trust?

Mrs. Entwhistle wished the ruby was back in its hiding place. She was half-tempted to put it there herself. She didn't need the aggravation, not to mention the shock of wondering if Floyd had a side to him she'd never imagined.

"I think you'd better see Butch about insuring it," Maxine said. "And then put it in your safety-deposit box at the bank. It's not safe to keep it here."

"Floyd kept it out in the tool shed for who knows how long." Mrs. Entwhistle fought a hysterical urge to laugh. "Max, I just can't figure it out. What was Floyd doing with such a valuable stone? Why hide it? How did he pay for it? What was he going to do with it? Was it an investment? Payment of a debt? Or a present? I can't imagine him giving me such a thing, so did he mean it for someone else?"

Maxine blinked. "Oh, now, Cora, you can't think Floyd...."

"Well, what else am I supposed to think? Jasmina saw a young man and a beautiful girl, their heads close together."

"Since when do you put any stock in what Jasmina sees?" Max asked.

~*~

She took the ruby to Butch at the insurance office and showed him the appraisal. He whistled, and then wrote up a policy for it. Mr. Dansinger at the bank whistled in the exact same way when she showed it to him. He personally pulled down her safety deposit box, wrapped the ruby in one of her old silk scarves, and put it within.

Then she went home and sat on the porch swing. She didn't weed, or cook, or ride her scooter. She barely acknowledged Roger, except to absently ruffle his ears. She was thinking. She was thinking that she needed to know more. More about rubies and more about Floyd.

There was plenty of information about rubies on the Internet. She learned that the Mogok Stone Tract in what was once Burma, now Myanmar, produces the finest rubies in the world—and the most expensive.

She found a folklore story on the website of one Richard W. Hughes:

"Long before the Buddha walked the earth, the northern part of Burma was said to be inhabited only by wild animals and birds of prey. One day the biggest and oldest eagle in creation flew over a valley. On a hillside shone an enormous morsel of fresh meat, bright red in color. The eagle attempted to pick it up, but its claws could not penetrate the blood-red substance. Try as he may, he could not grasp it. After many attempts, at last he understood. It was not a piece of meat, but a sacred and peerless stone, made from the fire and blood of the earth itself. The stone was the first ruby on earth and the valley was Mogok."

She shivered at the image of the blood-red stone mistaken for a meal by a bird of prey. The ruby seemed malevolent to her. It burned her eyes the first time she saw it and burned her peace of mind ever since.

What could any of this have to do with Floyd? Mrs. Entwhistle loved him loyally even in death, but she had to admit Floyd was the most phlegmatic of men. Steady, dependable, responsible—yes. A bold, swashbuckling smuggler of rubies? No. No way. He'd never been to Burma; he seldom left their small town.

Except... he had gone to Vietnam. His lottery draft number was ten, and he was soon called up. She remembered the day he left for boot camp. They were engaged, but Floyd had offered to release her from the engagement.

"We don't know if I'll come back," he said calmly, "or what kind of shape I'll be in if I do. I don't want you to waste your time waiting around. So I think we should break up for now and see what happens in a couple years."

She'd laughed at him and said, "Oh, go on, Floyd Entwhistle. As if I'd ever look at another man."

And Floyd had smiled and kissed her, and no more was said about breaking up.

He'd come home thinner, quieter, and troubled by nightmares, but he didn't talk about his experiences in Vietnam. He got a good job at the Bell Bomber plant, married her, and by the time the children came along, seemed to have stepped back into his pre-Army life. She'd never questioned him about what he'd been through; she figured if he wanted to talk about it, he would. Now she wished she'd pushed a little.

"There were plenty of men who had girlfriends while they were stationed overseas," she said to

Maxine. "For all I know, Floyd could have been one of them. He never talked about what happened over there, you know."

"I know, Jack didn't either," Maxine said. "But you're jumping to a crazy conclusion. Floyd would never have betrayed you. He was true-blue. I shouldn't have to remind *you* of that."

"But how do you explain that damn ruby?"

Maxine shook her head. "I can't. But I know someone who might could.

~*~

It took Booger a while to answer the door. He looked tousled and sleepy, like he'd just been awakened from a satisfying nap. He yawned hugely and scratched his chest.

"What d'ya want?"

"Manners, Booger, manners," Mrs. Entwhistle said. "I'm sorry we woke you. Would you rather we come back another time so you can continue your nap?"

"Naw, you're here and I'm awake now," Booger said ungraciously. "Set yourselves down. You want coffee or somethin'?"

"No, thank you, but you get yourself a cup. It'll help

you wake up."

Booger shuffled back into the house and was gone a long time. Mrs. Entwhistle and Maxine settled in the porch rockers after giving them a couple of flicks with their hankies. Housekeeping was not Booger's strong suit. When he returned, he was carrying a steaming cup of very black coffee and looked less disgruntled.

"Sorry I was short with y'all. Caleb says I'm always a bear when I first wake up. What's up?"

"You were in Vietnam at the same time Floyd was." Mrs. Entwhistle believed in getting to the point. "I need you to tell me what it was like over there. Not the battles," she added hastily, as Booger's face darkened. "I know you don't talk about that. But what was it like to go on leave? Did you and Floyd ever meet up? You know, two hometown boys?"

"Why you askin', after all these years?" he said. "What 'zackly are you drivin' at?"

So, Mrs. Entwhistle told him about the ruby, about Jasmina's vision of the beautiful girl, and about her doubts and fears. Booger listened without interrupting, his eyes on the horizon. When she ran out of words, he remained silent, rocking slowly back and forth. She was afraid he wasn't going to say anything, but then he spoke.

"Me 'n Floyd was in different units over there. We didn't keep in touch or nothin', there was too much goin' on. But once I did run into him in Hanoi. It was in a bar where all the G.I.s went. I heard a lot of noise comin' from a back room, and I took a look. There was a high stakes poker game goin' on, and Floyd was right in the middle of it."

"Floyd? I never knew him to play poker," Mrs. Entwhistle said.

"He didn't, not here at home. But over there... Well, we did a lotta stuff we wouldn't have done at home. So anyways, Floyd was playin' and there was all sorts at that table. He had a big ol' pile of chips in front of him. I recall his face was red as a beet." Booger looked down. "He'd had a little too much to drink, Cora."

She nodded. Words failed her at this portrait of Floyd drunk at a poker table on the other side of the world, a man she thought she knew as well as she knew herself, a man she'd have sworn couldn't surprise her. She didn't judge him; she could never walk in his shoes, and he wasn't around to explain.

Booger continued. "It was the last hand, and there was a big pile of chips in the center of the table.

Everybody folded but Floyd and one other guy, Asian feller. When they laid their cards down, Floyd had him a royal flush. That takes all," he explained for Mrs. Entwhistle's benefit. "The Asian, he looked mighty upset. He was shakin' his head and there was a lot of loud talkin' in a language we didn't unnerstand. Then he wrote somethin' on a scrap of paper and give it to Floyd."

"What did he write?" Mrs. Entwhistle asked. She felt like she was watching a movie starring a stranger.

"I don't rightly know. Floyd seen me then and he got up and come over. I asked him how much he won, and he said the guy was cleaned out, but he promised to send his sister to pay up the next day. Floyd said that'd prob'ly happen when pigs fly, but he didn't seem too upset about it. Then we had a beer and I had to go, 'cause I had to be back at camp at midnight."

"Do you think the man's sister might have given Floyd the ruby in payment for her brother's debt?"

"Coulda. There was a lot of smugglin' going' on, and you could buy them stones on the black market for cheap. If Floyd got a ruby, he mighta just stuck it away and forgot he even had it."

Mrs. Entwhistle thought of the dusty metal box in

the rafters of the tool shed. She thought of her husband, who had been drafted and sent to a foreign land when he was nineteen, where he fought for his country without a word of complaint. When he came home, he'd quietly worked his way through the bad memories and made a life. Floyd Entwhistle had been a good man. She'd known it then, and she knew it now.

She realized she faced a choice that could change her life, a choice she'd have to make right there on Booger's porch. She could continue to agonize over what may have happened, what could have happened, which Floyd was the true Floyd, who the beautiful girl was and what she gave to Floyd—all things Mrs. Entwhistle would never know. Or she could continue to rest her heart on what she did know: the solid foundation that she and Floyd had built. Fifty years of marriage, a family, a life. The path she chose was up to her.

She decided, and it wasn't hard. But she had one more question.

"Do you think I have a right to keep the ruby, or do I need to return it?" she asked, including Maxine in the question.

"I don't know who you'd return it to," Booger said. "It's more'n fifty years ago, and we don't even know if Floyd won it in that poker game. If he did, he won it fair and square. If he bought it some other time, then he paid what was asked. Either way, I'd say it's yours."

"Floyd would want you to have the money, even if you don't want the ruby," Maxine said.

Mrs. Entwhistle nodded noncommittally. She'd think about it. She had a feeling she'd think about it for a long time.

~*~

Mrs. Entwhistle tried to put the ruby out of her mind. She'd made her decision; the Floyd she knew was the Floyd she chose to cherish in memory. The other one, the young man who somehow came by a ruby worth half a million dollars and then hid it in the tool shed—well, no use speculating on why. She'd never know.

Young people make mistakes, she reflected. She'd certainly made her share. She remembered them all so clearly now that she was old. Nights when sleep didn't come, they would replay in her mind in a continuous loop. There were so many times she'd been ignorant, unperceptive, unkind. All she could do now was whisper, "I'm sorry," down the years.

If Floyd was here, he'd no doubt say he was sorry,

too. He'd always been good to own up to his mistakes; it was one of the things she loved about him. If the ruby *was* a mistake. It seemed to call questions from its resting place deep in the bank's vault. "Why am I here? Who was meant to have me? What are you going to do with me?"

She still hadn't told Tommy and Diane about finding the stone. It was part of their father's estate and thus their inheritance, so she'd want to get their approval before doing anything with it. Truthfully, she needed the money. Now that she was no longer working at the *Pantograph*, funds were tight. Mrs. Entwhistle wasn't greatly interested in money, but she did believe that the best gift she could give her children was her own financial independence. They had their own families to care for; she didn't want to be a burden.

At some point, she'd fall asleep during these midnight deliberations only to awaken more confused than ever. And not very rested, either. That ruby was like a big red stop-light on the highway of her life. Until she came to a resolution about it, she felt stuck.

But life has a way of moving on. The ruby was out of sight, and, as time passed, often out of mind. Mrs. Entwhistle got to where she'd go a full day without giving it a thought. So she was unprepared for the knock on her door on a sunny Saturday afternoon. A pair of dark-suited men stood on her porch. They wore black glasses that hid their eyes, and their hair was slicked straight back from their hairlines. Thing One and Thing Two, Mrs. Entwhistle immediately thought, minus the fluffy purple hair. She wondered if they'd brought the Cat in the Hat.

"Are you Cora Entwhistle?" one of them asked when she opened the door.

"Yes. What can I do for you?"

But her question went unanswered as the men pushed past her into the house, slamming her against the wall.

"Oof! What are you doing? You can't bust in here!"

"We're here for the ruby. Hand it over, and we'll be on our way."

"The ruby? What ruby?"

One of the men grabbed her arm and twisted it painfully behind her back. Her cry brought Roger snorkeling up from his nest of pillows on the sofa. The little dog's faculties were sadly reduced, but somehow, he heard the fear in her voice. He jumped to the floor, landing hard on his tummy with his legs splayed. Regaining his feet, he bit the nearest leg.

When the leg shook him off, Roger hit the wall with a yelp.

That cry cut through Mrs. Entwhistle's pain and fear. "Don't hurt him," she cried, "He can't hurt you. He's old."

"Damn little mutt bit me," Thing One said. "Shall we see if he can bounce? Or maybe you'd like to have one of his paws on your key chain? I'll bet you've got a sharp knife in the kitchen."

"No!" Mrs. Entwhistle screamed, and immediately capitulated. What did a stupid ruby matter measured against Roger? "Leave him alone! The ruby isn't here, but I can get it for you. Leave my dog alone, though, or you'll never see it."

"You ain't in no position to make threats," Thing Two said, giving her arm another twist. "Where's the ruby?"

"It's in my safe deposit box at the bank," Mrs. Entwhistle gasped. "And the bank's closed until Monday morning. Come back then, and I'll have it for you."

"You must think we're stupid," Thing One said. "We're not leaving you alone for a minute. You're coming with us." He marched her toward the door.

She saw a large van parked in her driveway and knew it was the vehicle in which they'd take her away. Wildly, she ran through the list of possible onlookers who might see them emerge from the house, and to whom she might signal. But Ronnie Sue and Biff, who lived next door, both worked on Saturdays. The across-the-street neighbors were building a deck in their back yard. The sound of power tools would drown out any cries she might make. The neighbors on the other side were on vacation, and her back yard blended into the woods. Saturday afternoon was turning out to be the ideal time for an unobserved kidnapping.

But before they reached the door, the mailman came into view, plodding steadily from house to house. The Things yanked Mrs. Entwhistle back into the living room. One of them pointed at Roger's nose, which showed from his hiding place under the sofa, while the other one clamped his hand over Mrs. Entwhistle's mouth.

"One peep and the dog has three legs," he hissed in her ear.

Mrs. Entwhistle stood motionless. They heard the mailman's footsteps approach, the rattle of the mail slot, and the footsteps retreat. The Things pushed her toward the door again, only to be stopped by another visitor.

This time it was Maxine. "Yoo-hoo, Cora! Why is your door locked? Are you home? I see your scooter. I'll go around back."

Thing One nodded at Thing Two, who moved soundlessly to the back door. As Maxine entered, he grabbed her in a choke hold and dragged her into the living room. Despite her thrashing and strangled cries, he controlled her easily. Maxine's frantic eyes sought Mrs. Entwhistle's, who shook her head and wordlessly conveyed the message: *don't fight, Max.* Maxine stopped struggling and nodded infinitesimally. Message received and understood. The two of them had communicated for so many years, words were not necessary.

Thing One produced zip-ties from his pocket and tied both women's hands behind their backs. Roughly, he pushed them down on the sofa, then knelt and tied Mrs. Entwhistle's left ankle to Maxine's right.

"Like a three-legged race," he said with a smirk. "Try running away now."

"We won't try to escape," Mrs. Entwhistle said. "I told you, I'll get the ruby first thing Monday morning when the bank reopens. But you need to let us go about our business until then. People will notice if we're not where we usually are."

The Things exchanged uneasy glances. "Where are you, usually?" one asked.

"I get my hair done every Saturday at three so it will look nice for church in the morning," Maxine said, "and Ronnie Sue will wonder what's wrong if I don't show up."

"And it's my turn to lead the Sunday School lesson," Mrs. Entwhistle said. "If I'm not there, everyone will notice. Plus, we take afternoon tea to the residents of the Shady Rest Assisted Living Center on Sunday. They look forward to it, and they'll surely want to know where we are if we don't show up."

"And my daughter, Geraldine, calls from Australia every Saturday evening. If I don't answer, she'll call the neighbors to check on me and make sure I'm all right."

Out in the street, the neighborhood kids started a game of baseball. Their cheerful shouts contrasted with the tense atmosphere in the house. The men regarded the ladies with narrowed eyes. One jerked his head toward the kitchen and the other one followed. Mrs. Entwhistle and Maxine heard their low voices in conference.

"Strategy meeting; they don't know what to do with us," Mrs. Entwhistle whispered. "LOLO, Max."

Maxine nodded as the Things returned, and One spoke. "Okay, it's too dangerous to leave with all those kids outside, so we're gonna stay right here until Monday morning. Call whoever you need to, so nobody'll come looking for you."

Two grabbed one of Roger's legs and drew him out of his hiding place. The little dog's eyes were ringed in white, and his teeth were bared in a snarl.

"It's okay, Roger," Mrs. Entwhistle said loudly. Roger couldn't hear very well. "It's okay, you're a good boy."

"He'll be a dead boy if you try anything funny on the phone. Now start calling."

Two tossed Mrs. Entwhistle's phone at her, but since her hands were secured behind her back, it bounced off her lap and skittered across the floor. One shot his partner a disgusted look. He picked up the phone and stood in front of Mrs. Entwhistle. "So who do you call about the Sunday School thing?"

"Jacinta. She's who I'd call about cancelling the tea party, too."

Two scrolled through her phone and found Jacinta's name. He tapped it, turned on Speaker, and held the phone in front of Mrs. Entwhistle's face. One gave Roger a painful poke that made him yelp. Any thoughts about sending a coded message to Jacinta flew out of Mrs. Entwhistle's head. Odds were, Jacinta wouldn't have gotten it, anyway. She wasn't the brightest headlight on the highway.

"Hello? Cora, is that you? Your name came up on my I.D. I just can't get over that I.D. thing. Isn't it neat?"

"Hi, Jacinta; yes, it's neat. Listen, I've got a little problem." Here One shot her a filthy look of warning. "I'm not feeling so well, and I don't want to take a chance of giving my germs to y'all tomorrow."

"Oh, do you think it's the flu?" Jacinta said, her voice apprehensive. She and all the residents of the Shady Rest were afraid of germs and viruses because, once introduced, they spread rapidly through their community.

"Well, I don't think so, but I can't take a chance. I won't be at church tomorrow, so could you take over the Sunday School lesson for me, and tell everyone at Shady Rest that afternoon tea is cancelled?"

"Of course, Cora, I'll put a note on the bulletin board in the dining room. I hope you feel better soon. Bye."

Jacinta broke the connection as though germs were crawling through the phone into her ear.

Mrs. Entwhistle raised her eyebrows. "Okay?" she

said to One.

"Yeah, I guess. Now, you." He gestured toward Maxine. "What's this haircut place?"

When he found Clip 'n Curl in Maxine's contact list, he held the phone to her face and she left a message when Ronnie Sue didn't pick up.

"Hi, honey, it's Maxine. I guess you're busy cutting hair right now. I'm sorry, but I can't keep my appointment this afternoon. I, uh, my car has a flat tire, and I have to wait for somebody from Bud's Garage to come and fix it. I'm sorry about the short notice."

Two nodded. "Now call your daughter."

"It's a call to *Australia*," Maxine said. "I use my land line at home when I call Geraldine because I can hear better. She'd wonder what was up if she saw a call come in from Cora's home phone. And I can't lie to Geraldine. She's got some kind of sixth sense about it; she hears it in my voice every time."

"Text her, then. Tell her your home phone is out of order and you can't talk to her this week. And don't try leaving no coded message, or the dog gets it."

Maxine did as she was told.

The Things dumped Roger on the floor and

retreated to the kitchen once again. Maxine and Mrs. Entwhistle had a few seconds to communicate.

"LOLO, Cora?"

"LOLO squared, Max!"

It was their private joke. LOLO stood for Little Old Lady Offensive, a tactic they trotted out when people were being particularly tiresome. LOLO meant dithering, obfuscating, losing the conversational thread in mid-sentence, and tottering in tiny, wobbly steps. LOLO called for cloudy confusion, endless stories about unknown people, opaque comprehension and trembling hands. There would be detailed descriptions of ailments and medications, and maybe a few tears. LOLO was like water on stone. It eventually reduced an annoying person to a quivering heap. It drove snotty receptionists mad, defeated door-to-door salesmen, and routed the most persistent recruiter of volunteers. Woe unto anyone else who called them little old ladies, but double-woe to those who caused them to unleash their secret weapon. They may have been wearing zip-ties at the moment, but they were not without resources. The thought of tormenting their tormenters was sweet.

One and Two returned from the kitchen eating jam sandwiches. Mrs. Entwhistle regretted the waste of her homemade strawberry jam on those two, but Maxine was 'way ahead of her. She gave Mrs. Entwhistle an "Aha!" look and fired the opening salvo of LOLO.

"Why, I bet you boys are hungry," she cooed. "Those little sandwiches aren't enough for two strong young men. Why don't you let us make you a real meal?"

Home-cooking, especially the kind they did, was a vanishing commodity in today's world. Mrs. Entwhistle and Maxine didn't know chiffonade from coulis, but they knew grits and gravy; they knew fried okra and fruit cobbler. Their food was evocative of home and comfort, and had been known to bring strong men to tears of nostalgia. As a LOLO weapon of distraction, it was unparalleled.

Mrs. Entwhistle jumped in. "Oh, that's a great idea. I love to cook, but it's too much trouble to make big meals just for myself. Now that I have some folks to cook for, I'd purely love to get in that kitchen."

"Cora, you could make your Swedish meatballs and gravy," Maxine said. "And I'll make mashed potatoes with sour cream and cream cheese and butter."

"Creamed corn!" Mrs. Entwhistle added. "Booger brought me some ears of fresh sweet corn. Oh, and I've got peaches. We can have peach cobbler."

The Things' eyes turned from one woman to the other as though they were watching a tennis match. They finished their sandwiches in one bite, but it was obvious that the menu descriptions were working on them.

"We ain't letting you loose just so's you can cook," One said, doubt in his voice. "Are we?" He turned to Two.

"No. I guess not...."

"But maybe if we just untied their hands...."

"They could still have their legs tied."

Maxine and Mrs. Entwhistle nodded like dashboard bobble heads. "Why, certainly, that would work," Maxine said.

But when their hands were free, they couldn't get to their feet despite flailing their arms and flinging themselves forward. The men finally grabbed them and heaved them upright in tandem.

"Oh! Oh!" Mrs. Entwhistle teetered and tottered, and Maxine did, too. "I don't believe I can keep my balance—Oh!" She sat back down abruptly, causing Maxine to do the same.

"We're just too old," Maxine said regretfully. "We have enough trouble staying upright on our own two feet. I'm afraid we can't do it with our legs tied together like this."

The Things made another trip to the kitchen to confer. Maxine and Mrs. Entwhistle exchanged a wink. When the men returned, Two said, "Look, you promise you won't make a run for it?"

"Why, how could we? We haven't run for years," Mrs. Entwhistle said.

"I've got your dog, remember," One said, looking around for Roger.

Roger was not to be seen. Mrs. Entwhistle knew he'd retreated to his special hiding-place, the one he went to only when life became unbearable. The guest room closet ran the length of one wall and was only four feet high, more of an attic than a closet. All manner of things were stuck in there, out of sight and out of Mrs. Entwhistle's mind. Roger sometimes ducked under the hanging clothes and crept all the way to the very end of the closet, where he curled up among the old boots for a restorative nap. The Things would never find him there, even if they went looking. It was a great relief to know her dog was no longer a bargaining chip.

"Now don't you worry. We promise we won't try to get away," Maxine said. "And by the way, you should tell us your names so we'd know what to call you. After all, you know ours."

"Youse don't need to know our names," Two said. "The less you know about us, the better."

"Okay, that's up to you, of course. We could just cook you some nice food, then. It'll help pass the time until Monday morning."

Two appeared to be thinking hard. "They're just little old ladies," he said, not hearing the jaws of their trap snap shut around him. "What could they possibly do, tied or untied? Anyway, I'm starving."

One agreed. The ankle ties were removed. The ladies made their way with tiny, tottering steps, into the kitchen. There was an extended search for aprons that involved opening and closing every door and drawer in the cabinets, some more than twice. Finally the aprons were found, shaken out and donned.

By then, Mrs. Entwhistle said she had to sit down and rest. "I declare, doesn't cooking make a person tired! Why, we haven't even started yet, and I'm just worn to a frazzle. Now this apron was my mama's, honey. She embroidered all these little flowers, see here? I recall her hands were stiff with the arthritis, but she worked at it every day as long as she could. I hate to wear such a pretty apron to cook, but I know she'd want me to. She'd say, 'Cora, now you go on and use that apron. That's what it's for.' She was the best mama, ya'll. Maxine, do you remember when she...."

Maxine not only remembered, it reminded her of a story about her own mama. Several tales later, Two's stomach gave such a loud rumble that it was clearly audible above the chatter.

"Why, you poor man, we'd better get you fed," Maxine said.

But now Mrs. Entwhistle had to go to the bathroom, which she announced in a ladylike whisper befitting the private nature of her mission.

"And me, too," Maxine whispered.

They puttered off in that direction, only to be blocked by Two. "You can't both go," he said. "One at a time."

Mrs. Entwhistle went first. It took a while. Quite a while. Then Maxine. When she finally emerged, waving her hands dry, Mrs. Entwhistle was again going through the cabinets searching for her cast-iron skillet. Maxine knew, and Mrs. Entwhistle knew, exactly where that skillet lived, but in LOLO Land, searches were maddeningly common and time-consuming. When the skillet was finally located, it proved to be too heavy for Mrs. Entwhistle's hand and fell to the floor with a thump.

"Oh, dear. Now I'll have to wash and season it before I can use it," she said. And that took a while, too.

Meanwhile, Maxine was examining every potato in the bin. One of them reminded her of her great-uncle Jess and she showed it to the Things. Then she sat down and told Uncle Jess's life story as well. Mrs. Entwhistle had to press her lips together to keep a straight face. There had never been an Uncle Jess. Max really should write fiction. Mrs. Entwhistle resolved to tell her so when all this was over.

Two had found a box of crackers and was stuffing them into his mouth by that time. Both men had despaired of ever having a meal.

But eventually the table was set and filled with mouth-watering food. The Things tucked in enthusiastically. Mrs. Entwhistle and Maxine kept it coming until both men pushed their chairs back from the table, groaning. Then Maxine brought out the peach cobbler and vanilla ice cream. By the time the orgy of eating was over, it was all One and Two could do to remain upright in their chairs. They stared at the wall while the ladies cleaned up the kitchen.

"Time for bed," Mrs. Entwhistle said. "Maxine and I will go upstairs and you men can—"

"Oh, no, you don't," Two said, suddenly alert. "You don't leave our sight."

"Well, in that case," Maxine said, "shall I take the sofa, Cora, and you the recliner?"

"Yes, that's fine. I'll get blankets and pillows." Which she did, accompanied by One.

Both ladies made nests in their respective places and settled down comfortably. "Nighty-night," they called.

One quickly took the only seat left in the room, a stiff-backed wing chair. Two dragged in a straight dining room chair, and both of them sat holding their distended bellies. No matter how hard they fought it, sleep was inevitable. When their heads had dropped to their chests for the final time and snoring filled the room, Mrs. Entwhistle opened her eyes. Maxine was already emerging from her cocoon of blankets. Carefully, Mrs. Entwhistle lowered the footrest of Floyd's old recliner. It tended to release with a loud thump if you weren't careful. The women stood.

"Floor squeaks," Mrs. Entwhistle mouthed. She inclined her head. "Follow me."

She led them on a circuitous route around the squeaking floorboards. They had almost gained the kitchen and were heading for the back door when thumping and yelping shattered the silence. Roger had emerged from his hiding place and come in search of his belated dinner. In the dark, he'd lost his footing and tumbled down the stairs. Mrs. Entwhistle darted to him, but it was too late. One and Two snorted and raised their heads.

"Hey! You two get back here!" The men scrambled to their feet.

"Roger needs his supper," Mrs. Entwhistle said, picking him up.

"It don't take two to do that. You, Maxine, you get back here."

Maxine shrugged and returned to the sofa.

The rest of the night passed uneventfully. To their surprise, both Maxine and Mrs. Entwhistle slept. Not as well as they would have done in their own beds, but well enough to allow them to feel alert and rested when dawn came. The Things had stretched out on the floor by then. Mrs. Entwhistle and Maxine stepped over them as delicately as possible, but it was enough to rouse Two. He moaned and levered himself to his feet, kicking his partner as he did so.

"They're on the move," he rasped. "Wake up."

'I'll put some coffee on," Mrs. Entwhistle said. "And then I'll make you a nice breakfast."

~*~

The Things rubbed their faces and ran their tongues over their furry teeth. This mission wasn't going at all as they'd planned. When Mr. Lacey hired them, he said it would be like taking candy from a baby to get the ruby from Mrs. Entwhistle. They hadn't even done a recon before knocking on her door because it was supposed to be such a piece of cake. Just shake her up enough to scare her, then collect the gem and scram.

Nobody mentioned the possibility of the ruby being in a safe-deposit box, nor that a hick small-town bank closed its doors at noon on Saturday. Sure as hell nobody mentioned they'd have to hold two little old ladies hostage from Saturday afternoon until Monday morning. This wasn't the first job they'd done for that arrogant creep, Lacey, but they agreed it would be the last. Some things just weren't worth the money.

The next twenty-four hours stretched ahead like a threat.

~*~

It took the ladies ages to cook, serve and clean up breakfast. All their twittery little starts and stops were exhausting to watch. Finally, the Things zip-tied the back door shut and retreated to the living room. Turning on the television, they sought in vain for a program that was not a church service. The sound of hymns filled the house, and Maxine sang along from the kitchen.

"Oh, come to the church in the wildwood, come to the church in the dell."

Mrs. Entwhistle harmonized in her clear soprano: "No spot is so dear to my childhood as the little brown church in the dell."

Two was astonished to hear One join in with a robust bass. "Oh, come, come, come, come to the church in the wildwood...."

He snapped his mouth shut when he saw Two's incredulous face and blushed a fiery red. "My Mom sang that one all the time," he muttered.

"Your mother must have been a lovely person," Maxine said from the kitchen doorway. Her voice was soft. "Did she take you to church and Sunday School when you were a boy?"

"Oh, yeah. If the church doors were open, Mom was there."

"Is she still living?"

"No."

"I guess you miss her."

"I don't wanna talk about my mom." One's voice was thick.

"Some people think the departed can see us. Do you suppose your mom is watching you right now?"

One's chair flew backward as he crossed the room to Maxine in two strides. He grabbed her by the shoulders. "You shut your mouth about my mom!" he screamed in her face.

Maxine regarded him tenderly. "It's okay," she said. "It's okay. Your mom loves you, no matter what."

One's arms dropped and his head followed. Without a word, he turned and walked out of the house. Two watched him go, mouth open.

"What the hell?" he said. "What's got into him?"

"He's just thinking about how things were when he was a boy, and how different his life is now," Maxine explained. "It upsets him."

"Yeah? Quit getting him upset, then."

Hearing it all from the kitchen, Mrs. Entwhistle

smiled. You wouldn't expect a tough guy to have such thin skin. Not surprising that LOLO was beginning to get under it. She looked out the window and saw One shambling around the backyard. With his rumpled black suit and slicked back hair, he looked as out of place as a giraffe. *Good*, she thought. *If the neighbors notice him, they'll be curious about what he's doing here.*

The remainder of the day seemed to stretch out forever. Conversation was sporadic, not only because the men didn't want to talk, but also because LOLO dictated tedious monologues. Mrs. Entwhistle's throat felt raw after hours of non-stop, tinkly talk. One good thing was that the Things seemed to have forgotten Roger. There were no more threats to amputate his paws or bounce him off the walls. On his part, he'd returned to his usual sleepy somnolence.

Maxine was up to something, though. Mrs. Entwhistle had known her long enough to recognize the signs. After One returned to the house, Max made a point of sitting near him and talking quietly. One tried to ignore her, but couldn't help responding to her sympathetic voice and eyes. A couple of times he wiped his hand over his face and looked furtively at his partner.

He misses his mother, Mrs. Entwhistle thought, and

feels guilty about being a criminal. Maxine is playing on that. She decided to devote her attention to Two. That turned out to be a different matter.

Two was the older of the men, and he was a hard case. Mrs. Entwhistle's questions about his past life were met with silence. Apparently Two had no tender memories of childhood that she could stir. She tried another tactic.

"It must be exciting to live a life of... crime, I guess... like yours."

"Oh, yeah, more fun than a roller coaster," Two muttered, cleaning his fingernails with his pocket knife.

"One thing I've been wondering. How did you know about my ruby? I didn't tell anyone except my banker, and insurance agent, and the appraisers—oh, I bet it was that Mr. Lacey wasn't it? He sent you to steal my ruby, didn't he?"

"Look, old lady, it don't matter who told me to do what. That ruby is leaving with me. That's all you need to know."

"I think it might be bad luck, you know. It's caused me nothing but trouble since I found it. Would you like to hear the story of how I came by it?"

"Nope. I don't care. Just hand it over Monday morning and you'll never see me again."

"My conscience tells me I ought to warn you about something," Mrs. Entwhistle said, giving Two a shy, sideways glance. "It's just that I feel somehow responsible for you. You're a guest in my house, sort of, and well, I'd hate to see you get hurt."

"Oh, yeah? Who's gonna hurt me?"

"I have a friend who's a Federal lawman."

"What?" Two sat up at attention. "What kinda lawman?"

"He's a Deputy United States Marshall and a good friend. In fact, Marshall Peters often drops by to check on me. If he finds you here...Well, I feel like I know you boys now, and I'd hate to see you get in trouble. You could leave now, and no harm done. We wouldn't report you. You're so young; it would be a shame if you went to prison."

"It wouldn't be the first time, but I don't plan to go back. I'd rather die."

"Maybe it *would* be better if you just left, never mind the ruby."

"Oh, no you don't. You ain't talking us out of it that easy. Old Man Lacey would have our guts on a stick."

"Ah, so it was Mr. Lacey."

"Nah, you didn't hear me right. I said Mr., uh, Hasty."

Mrs. Entwhistle nodded and smiled trustingly at Two. She'd sowed seeds of worry and she could see they were taking root in his mind. He couldn't sit still, walking from window to window, rattling the change in his pocket, picking up her knick-knacks and putting them down.

"Jeez, take a chill pill, will 'ya?" One said. "You're driving me nuts."

"Oh, yeah? Did you know this one here has a friend who's a U.S. Marshall? Says he checks on her often."

That brought One to his feet, and both men paced through the house. They reminded Mrs. Entwhistle of caged tigers she'd seen at the zoo. She knew Pete Peters was out of town, but even the suggestion of his presence scared these two. She let them stew.

Meanwhile, Mrs. Entwhistle and Maxine kept themselves busy. First, they dusted. Every object was handled and discussed, its story told. They made endless cups of tea to keep their throats lubricated as they talked. And talked. And talked. Sometimes they shot each other surprised glances that said, *Is that true? Or made up for the moment?* There'd be a lot of debriefing when this was all over.

Then they cooked. Cookies and scones to go with the tea. An elaborate meatless meal composed of vegetables from Mrs. Entwhistle's garden. Fried green tomatoes, roasting ears, stuffed peppers, and sautéed green beans were accompanied by cathead biscuits dripping with butter. The Things kept emptying the plates that Mrs. Entwhistle kept refilling until they'd eaten themselves into another food coma. Again, they were miserably stuffed and in need of a nap.

"Geez, you'd think we woulda learned," One said. "I can't stay awake. Let's tie 'em back up so we can sleep a minute."

It was clear that sleep was a rolling tide against which resistance was futile. The Things directed Mrs. Entwhistle and Maxine to sit on the sofa and zip-tied their ankles together again.

"Can we trust youse to sit still if we don't tie your hands?" Two asked.

"You know we can't get up with our ankles tied together," Mrs. Entwhistle said. "You saw how that went before, remember? We'll just sit here and chat while you boys have yourselves a little snooze."

"I'm sure you didn't sleep well on the floor last night," Maxine said in a concerned voice.

"That's the understatement of the year," Two said.

The men loosened their belts and stretched out, groaning. The heavy drag of sleep pulled at them. Gentle chatter ran together into a lullaby. They slept.

When their snores reached a suitable decibel level, Maxine drew a needle-nosed pliers from her apron pocket. Mrs. Entwhistle recognized the tool as part of the small kit Floyd had kept in the pantry. Maxine had spent some time in there during their cooking spree, rummaging around for various ingredients, but she'd never hinted at what she'd found. She marveled at her friend's poker-faced composure and reflected for the thousandth time that there never was a better friend than Maxine.

Now Max snipped away at the plastic tie around their ankles until it snapped. Mrs. Entwhistle blessed her late husband's insistence on always having good tools.

Freed, the women tiptoed to the front door and let themselves out. Mrs. Entwhistle turned the old-fashioned lock with the big iron key. When the Things awoke and discovered the ladies missing, they'd race to the front door and find themselves locked in. Then they'd run to the back door, but they'd have to stop and remove the zip-tie. It would take them a few minutes, and that might be just the time the ladies needed to complete their escape.

Maxine headed straight for the black SUV, took the needle-nose pliers from her pocket and knelt at the front left tire. Expertly, she inserted the pliers into the air valve and removed the stem. The tire hissed gently as it deflated. She moved to the other side and repeated the procedure. Mrs. Entwhistle watched in awe. *Where had Maxine learned to do that?*

As the tires sighed into a deflated puddle on the driveway, the ladies walked over the lawn to Ronnie Sue's house. She and Biff were sitting on the front porch.

"Well, hi, you two," Ronnie Sue said. "Come on up and sit. We thought you had company."

"We need to use your phone, honey, to call the police."

"What's wrong?"

"There are two men in my house that need to be arrested," Mrs. Entwhistle said.

Ronnie Sue knew her neighbor. She asked no more questions, handed over her cell phone and sat back to watch what happened next.

What happened next were two black-suited, slick-haired city boys bursting out the back door of Mrs.

Entwhistle's house.

"Hey, youse two! Get back here!" Thing One shouted, seeing Mrs. Entwhistle and Maxine on the neighboring porch.

Thing Two ran for the car, stopping short when he saw the flat front tires. "Come on," he yelled to his partner. "We gotta get out of here. We'll drive on the rims."

In the distance, a siren announced the approach of the law. The men turned and made for the woods, but Ronnie Sue's big orange tom-cat chose that moment to greet the newcomers.

Mrs. Entwhistle was convinced that cat had a sixth sense for when he wasn't wanted, and inevitably showed up. She watched as he wound around the legs of Thing One, causing him to stumble into Two. Both men went down in a heap as the cat, with an indignant yowl, leaped clear and stalked away, tail swishing. By now, the sheriff and his deputy were jumping from their vehicle and running toward the Things, who had enough sense to know it was all over. Resignedly, they got to their feet and raised their hands.

~*~

Thing One and Thing Two had no compunctions

about turning on their boss. In fact, they struck a deal with the district attorney: for their help in uncovering a network of gem thieves, they'd receive a reduction of the charges against them, with the most important one, kidnapping, dropped. They'd go to prison, but not for life, and they'd have the satisfaction of knowing that James Lacey would be locked up, too.

~*~

The Burmese ruby lay quiescent in the dark box in the bank vault. No ray of light illuminated its crimson depths, and without light, it was simply a lifeless red stone. Until the day it would again reflect fire from the sun, it rested quietly. It had been around for millennia. It could wait.

~*~

The sirens woke Mrs. Entwhistle. Groggily, she saw that the big red numbers on her bedside clock said 3:31 A.M. She rose to peer out the window and saw flashing lights clustered on Main Street. Rapidly, her mind catalogued the businesses there: bank, Busy Bee Diner, *Pantograph* office, Clip 'n Curl, Hallmark, Bud's Garage, Garibaldi's Hardware, Daily Diner, Mack's Shoe Repair, Walgreens, Rub-a-Dub Pub and Washateria. Main Street was a short street and at this time of night, deserted. Whatever was going on, the people who worked there would be safe at home in their beds.

Sleep was over for that night, so she made a cup of tea and headed for the porch swing, cell phone in hand. Someone would be calling her with the news. Before she even got herself settled, the phone rang.

"Cora, are you awake? Do you hear the sirens?"

It was Maxine.

"Yes, I'm out on the porch. I can see the flashing lights from here. Do you know what's going on?"

"There's a fire in the bank. Firemen are swarming all over the building."

Maxine had an unimpeded view of Main Street from her upstairs window. Mrs. Entwhistle knew that's where she was, wrapped in her warm robe, wearing her favorite floppy bunny slippers that were an accident waiting to happen.

Mrs. Entwhistle thought of her safe deposit box in the vault and its contents, the Burmese ruby. "It's that ruby. It's bad luck, Max, and now it has set the bank on fire."

"Oh, come on, Cora, no stone can do that. Let's just wait and see what the fire chief says."

What he said on the early morning news was that a fire of unknown origin broke out in the vault of the bank. The heat set off the alarm and the volunteer fire department responded with their customary speed and efficiency.

"No one was hurt and damage to the vault was minimal," the chief said. "Mr. Dansinger said it will be business as usual today, and the staff will be happy to help you check on your safe deposit boxes."

Mrs. Entwhistle snorted. She wouldn't bother checking hers. It was where the fire started, and she knew that sure as shooting. The Burmese ruby was tired of being cooped up in the dark. It wanted out. Mrs. Entwhistle shuddered. It was her stone, so it was her problem to solve. If only she knew how. If only she knew more.

In a quest for knowledge, she turned again to the Internet for further information about Myanmar, formerly Burma, where the stone originated. The pictured populace seemed to be exceptionally good-looking, especially the children, and the scenery was beautiful, including the Mogok Valley where her ruby was mined. But there was no escaping the poverty. Despite its resource of precious stones, Myanmar was one of the poorest countries in that part of the world.

She saw photographs of traders on the streets of Rangoon, selling rubies from Mogok Valley for whatever they could get. She shook her head when she read that some called Burmese rubies "genocide gems." Mrs. Entwhistle wished again that she'd never seen the malevolent red stone smoldering in the bank vault. To think she actually owned such a thing!

And then she came upon the pictures of the children.

Their faces were both resigned and hopeful, pleading mutely for strangers to change their lives. "Waiting 430 days...waiting 350 days...waiting 190 days..." the captions above their pictures said. She knew many would wait forever for help that never came.

There was one young woman whose face called to her from the screen. Her name was Pattamyar, and her thumbnail biography said she was seventeen and had been an orphan since the age of six, when her village was overrun by militia.

"Pattamyar has completed primary, lower secondary and upper secondary classes, in which she excelled. Her dream is to become a physician. 'I want to give back to my country, and my country needs doctors,' Pattamyar says."

Mrs. Entwhistle looked at Pattamyar's photograph for a long time. She saw an intelligent, lively face, eyes that met the camera straight on, and an unmistakable glint of steely determination.

What if I could make this girl's dream come true? I bet the ruby would just about pay for medical school. Think of the good she'd do for so many others. But how would I go about sponsoring her for such a venture? It wouldn't be just a matter of buying her school uniforms and sending care packages. This would be a long-term, huge, financial commitment. How could I be sure the money was getting to the medical school, not lining the pockets of corrupt officials? I wish I could talk this over with someone who knows how things work over there.

She could do more research, she supposed. Or maybe get in touch with the Myanmar embassy, wherever that was. Or...Wait! She could pay a call on Kiki and Aung Cho. Kiki was a second-generation American, but her father was a naturalized citizen, and he would hold a wealth of knowledge about his homeland.

~*~

Settled comfortably with Aung Cho and Kiki in the back room of their shop, Mrs. Entwhistle and Maxine sipped their tea. Mrs. Entwhistle fought her inclination to get right to the purpose of her visit. She'd learned her friends preferred a more leisurely approach to conversation.

Mrs. Entwhistle had never told Aung Cho and Kiki the story behind the Burmese ruby, and she told it now. She spoke of its discovery, hidden by her late husband so long ago; the seeds of doubt about how and why he came to have it, her reluctance to profit from it, and her belief that the stone brought her bad luck. She related the visit by Things One and Two, who'd been sent to steal the stone, and ended with the fire in the bank vault.

"Now I can't prove the ruby started the fire, and Maxine says I'm being fanciful, but I can't be convinced otherwise," Mrs. Entwhistle said. "The ruby has brought me nothing but worry and danger."

Kiki's eyes were wide, but Aung Cho didn't look surprised. He only nodded.

"So, I was thinking of how the ruby could be used to do some good in the world. I saw a photograph of a young Myanmar girl named Pattamyar, who wants to become a doctor."

Here she stopped, because Kiki and her father were exchanging astonished glances.

"What is it? What did I say?"

"You say the girl's name is Pattamyar?" Aung Cho asked.

"Yes, that's what it said on the website. I'm probably not pronouncing it right."

"That is not a common name for a child."

"Why not? Does it have some special meaning?"

"All Burmese names have meaning. This one, Pattamyar, means ruby."

They thought about this in silence. Maxine was the one to speak first.

"I don't believe in coincidence," she said, "so if this girl's name means ruby, and Cora has a ruby to offer her...Well, it's a sign. It's meant to be, that's all."

"I'm not going to risk half a million dollars on the strength of a name," Mrs. Entwhistle said decisively. "There are a zillion practical details to work out first. For starters, how do we know this girl isn't a scammer trying to get rich quick? Aung Cho, I don't know how to verify her story. What can I do?"

"Ah, you must leave that to me, dear Mrs. Entwhistle. I still know many people in Myanmar, including the head of this orphanage. It's a small country in terms of helping agencies. So I will contact her, we will have a conversation in our first language, Burmese, where we understand each other perfectly, and I will verify Pattamyar's story."

"If her story is true..." He paused for a moment, then continued meditatively, almost as though he was talking to himself. "Then she must receive her medical education in the United States. Given her grades, there should be no difficulty in getting into a good school. She will live with us. Kyi Kra and I will become her new father and sister, and Daw Cora and Daw Maxine will be her honored grandmothers. I can easily sell the Burmese ruby and see that it brings top dollar. Along with scholarships, there should be enough to cover medical school."

He beamed at Mrs. Entwhistle. "You are not to worry about details. How do they say it here? I got this!"

Mrs. Entwhistle didn't tell anyone, not even Maxine, that she was having second and third thoughts. She was ashamed that she was not immune to the temptations of wealth, but she was old enough to know that while money wasn't the most important thing, it was a close second. The ruby was worth a fortune. Was she right to give it away? Was that what Floyd would have wanted? Or was she being naïve and short-sighted, risking becoming a burden to her children if she couldn't meet her own financial needs? She spent a restless night debating these points with herself. When she rose at dawn, she knew she needed to see the ruby again. Maybe laying eyes on it would clear her mind.

She was waiting outside the bank when Mr. Dansinger opened the doors.

"Why, Mrs. Entwhistle, come inside. Why didn't you call me? I'd have opened the bank early for you. Please, sit down. Coffee? Tea? Jake, would you please fetch a cup of tea for Mrs. Entwhistle? Two sugars. Thanks. Now what can I do for you this morning?"

"I just feel I need to see that ruby again. I know the vault is still being cleaned up, and I'm sorry to bother you at a time like this. Especially since the ruby was the cause of the fire."

"We don't know that," Mr. Dansinger protested. "It started near your safe deposit box, but we still don't know why. Maybe it was an electrical short. You mustn't worry about it; no great harm was done, and the vault needed a good cleaning, anyway. I'll bring your box into my office and you can open it there in privacy."

Mrs. Entwhistle was ensconced behind Mr.

Dansinger's desk, and her sooty safe deposit box was placed on the blotter before her. She took a deep breath before reaching out to turn the key and raise the lid.

The ruby had somehow come unwrapped and lay upon its nest of silk radiating crimson splendor. Picking it up, she held it in her palm, closed her eyes and felt its warmth and weight and worth. She sat quietly for a few minutes, breathing evenly. Then, slowly, she opened her eyes and her hand.

"You've caused me enough heartache," she said softly. "Whatever Floyd's reasons were for bringing you home, I think he'd like to know that now you're going to do some good in this world. I don't believe I need you after all. Not one bit."

Later, Mrs. Entwhistle conceded that there might have been a flicker from the overhead light, or perhaps a shaft of sunshine penetrated the window at just that moment. Maybe her eyesight was blurry from unshed tears. But, she insisted, she saw what she saw.

The Burmese ruby winked.

Mrs. Entwhistle and the Big Box Store

Mrs. Entwhistle realized she'd forgotten a crucial part of the decorations for Lara's baby shower. She could hardly believe the young couple was expecting a baby already. Seemed to her they'd just gotten married and had barely settled themselves in Washington, D.C., where Dex worked for the Washington Post. And now their first child was on the way. What a lot was going on in their lives! It made her tired just thinking about it, but they were young and in love, and had energy to spare. She smiled; thinking about Dex always made her smile.

Mrs. Entwhistle cast a critical eye over the table. Since Lara planned to decorate the nursery in seaside décor, Mrs. Entwhistle was extending the theme to the shower. She'd picked an armful of fresh zinnias from her garden and arranged them in little tin sand pails; the miniscule shovels and rakes she'd found at the dollar store were scattered around the table; she'd even stumbled on coral-printed fabric to make the tablecloth and napkins. But she'd forgotten the child-size paper parasol she wanted to prop like a beach umbrella behind the cake, the one she'd spent all day baking and decorating.

Now it was nearing eight p.m., and she was ready to put her feet up. Groaning, she realized she'd have to make a trip to the store. And not just the corner store, either; it would have to be the big box store beside the interstate. She'd seen parasols there and for a good price, too. Why, oh, why hadn't she picked one up at the time?

Mrs. Entwhistle paused to think. In the morning, she'd be busy putting the last-minute finishing touches on lunch. Twenty ladies would be arriving at noon with prettily-wrapped packages and powerful appetites. She had to be ready.

Glancing at the clock, she realized Maxine would already be in her p.j.'s, watching television with one eye shut, ready for bed. She couldn't ask her to get dressed and drive her to the store. There were limits to what you could ask even of a life-long friend. With a sigh, she realized there was nothing to do but make the run herself on her scooter. She'd never driven it on the interstate, but desperate times called for desperate measures. Fortunately, it was summer and the light wouldn't fade for another hour. She could do it, she decided with her usual self-confidence.

Grabbing her shoulder bag, she stooped to pat Roger. "I'll be back in a jiffy," she told the little dog. Roger blinked up at her and wagged his tail a couple of times. Then he went back to sleep.

The interstate drive was fully as terrifying as she'd expected. Huge trucks roared by with such a backwash she had to hold on tight to her handlebars. Tailgating drivers laid on their horns, infuriated by her modest speed. She received the middle finger salute and was too demoralized to return her usual cheery wave. Limp with rattled nerves, she nosed her scooter into a parking space and made her way to the store's entrance.

Mrs. Entwhistle entered the Bargain Barn at 8:15 p.m. The greeter at the door checked her membership card and warned her that the store would be closing in forty-five minutes.

"No problem," she said, "I've just got a quick errand."

But nothing in the Bargain Barn ever happened quickly. There was an acre of ground to cover. She pushed her cart down aisle after aisle, trying to remember where she'd seen the parasols. On Aisle

17, she was suddenly overtaken by an urgent need to visit the bathroom.

Oh, dear! It's that Diet Coke I've been drinking all afternoon. Where's the Ladies?

Of course, it was at the opposite end of the store, and she hurried toward it. As she entered, the cleaning lady was exiting, pushing her cart of supplies.

"Be careful," the cleaner said, "I just mopped this floor. I didn't put any wet floor signs out because we're closing in a few minutes. You might be the last customer. You do know we're about to close, don't you?"

"I know, I know. I'll hurry, and I'll be careful."

Mrs. Entwhistle hurried, then stepped quickly to the sink to wash her hands. She thought later she must have slipped in a spot of water. Her feet flew out from under her, and her head thumped on the floor. The lights went out for her, and a few moments later the lights went out in the store.

The first thing she became aware of was the pain in her head. That and the velvety darkness that enveloped her. It didn't seem to matter much whether her eyes were open or closed.

Mrs. Entwhistle lay very still for a couple of minutes, checking herself mentally from head to toe. She cautiously moved her arms and legs, wiggling her fingers and toes. Everything seemed to be working. Slowly, she sat up, touching the large bump that was already forming on the back of her head.

She remembered she was in the Bargain Barn, specifically in the ladies' room, and more specifically, on the floor.

Thank goodness the floor was just mopped; at least it's clean. You'd think they'd have some kind of security light in here. It's as dark as the inside of a goat.

That's what Floyd had always said, and she'd never failed to inquire how he knew the degree of darkness inside of a goat. Groping, she found the edge of the sink and used it to pull herself up. She felt better once she was on her feet. Keeping one hand on the wall, she managed to find the door.

There was a dim, yellowish light in the store itself. Surely, there would be people around—cleaners, stockers, security guards—someone who could help her. She listened for the sound of voices, but heard nothing. Her cart was still parked outside the restroom and she used it to steady herself as she walked toward the exit. There were six double doors, and she pushed on all of them.

Locked tight.

Okay, time to call for reinforcements. Mrs. Entwhistle pulled out her phone. Dead. Drat! She'd had that long conversation with Jacinta that afternoon. There was no other kind of conversation you could have with Jacinta, no matter how much you struggled and said you had to go; long was all Jacinta knew.

There are phones in the store. I'll find one and call for help.

But the ones behind the counters were internal phones only; they didn't have outside lines.

I'll go to the office.

Locked double-tight.

I'll yell!

But the sound of her voice echoing in the eerie, yellow-lit store was so disconcerting she didn't try it but once.

There's got to be a back door the employees use, or a loading dock. There should be people there unloading stock for tomorrow.

She set off again in the deserted aisles. Hurry up, she

admonished herself, but she felt like she was wearing concrete boots. When she came to a furniture display, the sofa beckoned irresistibly. It was piled with plump pillows and there was a fuzzy throw flung over the back. Mrs. Entwhistle felt pulled toward it like an iron filing to a magnet.

I'll just sit down for a minute.

She woke three hours later.

By now, it was past midnight. She wondered what Roger thought. He'd never been alone in the house at night.

But, knowing Roger, he's sound asleep. He's the least of my worries. I've got to get out of here. There are all those ladies to feed tomorrow.

Even in her difficult circumstances, she felt a tingle of joy at the thought of the shower and the reason for it. Dex and Lara's first baby! The child would be like a grandbaby to her, just as Dex and Lara seemed like her own children.

Now that they'd moved to Washington, their trips to see her were infrequent and would be even more so after the baby arrived. When they did come, they refused to stay at her house because Dex worried it was too much work for her. She'd barely got him to agree that she could give Lara a shower.

"Remember, Mrs. E., you're almost eighty now," Dex said. "You have to take care of yourself."

He was a sweet boy, Dex was. But now she had to pull herself together and get out of this store. Rising from the sofa, she plumped the pillows and re-draped the throw. Her head gave a decided thump, and a stabbing pain traveled down her left leg. She had to admit she felt a bit unsteady on her feet.

Well, that's to be expected. I hit the floor pretty hard. Sure wish I had my cane. Wait, I'm in a store; I'll pick one up and pay for it later.

She resumed her trek through the aisles. While she was at it, she might as well look for what she came to buy, so she peered through the dim light for parasols and canes. *Aha! There were the parasols.* There were only two left of the big display she remembered. She grabbed one. Not the prettiest and a little tattered, but it would have to do.

She walked down a corridor marked "Staff Only." Here, at last, was the back door that presumably led to the loading dock. It, too, was locked. She pressed her ear against the steel, straining to hear signs of life on the other side, but she heard only silence. She banged on the door and shouted, but there was no response. Maybe the unloading didn't happen until closer to morning.

Might as well locate the canes, then, before she had another fall. She headed toward the pharmacy, thinking medical supplies, including canes, would be close by. The metal grill was down over the counter where drugs were dispensed, but there was an end-cap display of canes. She grabbed one and tried it out. Yes, much better.

From the corner of her eyes, she caught a movement behind the grille. Freezing in place, she waited and watched. There it was again. Straining her eyes, she peered through the yellow light. Instinct told her not to call out until she had some idea who was back there. An employee would have turned on the lights, would have made some noise. But all was quiet and dark.

A flashlight's thin beam traveled along the shelves of medicines. A hand reached out and grabbed a bottle of pills, knocking others to the floor. Mrs. Entwhistle was sure she was watching a robbery in progress.

She wasn't overly concerned about any losses to the Bargain Barn, now at the very bottom of her list of favorite stores. Served 'em right, them and their wet floors, was what she thought. But maybe if she watched, she could see how he'd gotten in, and when the coast was clear, she could leave the same way. The burglar tipped the bottle of pills into his hand and popped some into his mouth. She heard a long sigh.

Maxine would have scolded her for impatience, but Mrs. Entwhistle wanted to go home. She had a big day tomorrow and needed to get some sleep in her own bed. Besides, she wanted to be up bright and early to make cheese straws. Timed right, they'd come out of the oven five minutes before the first guest arrived. The aroma would put everyone in a party mood.

So, phooey on spending any more time in this darn store. I've got things to do.

"Hey, there, you! Stop where you are. I've got a gun, and the police are on the way," she called.

Her naturally loud voice echoed in the quiet store. The burglar jumped and whirled around in the direction of the sound. "Don't shoot! I give up."

There was no mistaking the soprano. The burglar was a girl.

Mrs. Entwhistle advanced to the metal grille. She looked over at the slight figure on the other side. "How did you get in?" she demanded. "Why are you here?"

"Why are *you* here?" the girl demanded, with some spirit. "You don't have any more business here than I do. I bet you're robbing the place."

"Oh, for heaven's sake!" Mrs. Entwhistle thumped the cane on the floor. "Look at me. Do I look like a burglar?"

"Well, do I?" the girl responded.

She had a point. She looked like a high school student. Appearing remarkably relaxed, the girl leaned on the counter and rested her head on the metal grille that separated them.

Mrs. Entwhistle feared she might slide to the floor. "Here!" she said, thumping the cane again. "You straighten up and stay awake. What did you just swallow, anyway?"

"Oh, just some oxy. You want some?"

"Certainly not. How did you get into the store? Are you alone?"

"I'm alone. 'I'm a lonesome polecat, lonesome, saaaaad and blue.'"

The girl was singing. She was a singing burglar. Mrs. Entwhistle felt an urge to giggle. She could see the newspaper headline now: "Senior Citizen and Singing Burglar trapped in Bargain Barn." She'd finally retired from her job as reporter for the *Pantograph*, but she still thought in headlines at

Doris Reidy

times. Such an article would be above the fold on the front page, for sure. The thought of what her former editor, Jimmy Jack McNamara, would say made her laugh out loud.

The girl heard her and laughed, too. "Good f' you, old lady. Better to laugh than cry, right? And you don't even have these nice pills to make you happy."

"Listen, what's your name?"

"What's yours? You tell me yours, and I'll tell you mine."

"I am Mrs. Entwhistle."

"I'm Mia. Me-me-me-ah."

"Mia, tell me how you got into the store. I need to get out. Maybe we can help each other."

"I came down through that cold-air return vent," Mia said, gesturing above her. Mrs. Entwhistle could make out the grate hanging by its hinges from the ceiling. "I just climbed up the fire escape 'til I was up on the roof and wiggled down here. 'When this old world starts getting me down....'"

"Stop that singing. You're too young to know the words to golden oldies."

"My Gran an' me used to sing while we did the

224

dishes."

"What would your Gran say if she saw you now?"

"Prob'ly say, 'Mia, I'm not mad, I'm just real disappointed.'"

"What about your parents?"

"Don't got any. They left me with Gran a long time ago. I didn't care; I liked it with Gran. She was better'n them anyway."

"And where is Gran now?" Mrs. Entwhistle had a feeling she already knew.

"Gran's in the ground now." Mia put her hands over her face and burst into noisy tears. "She's in the ground, and it's cold 'n dark, an' she always hated to be cold. I can't stand to think she's cold."

"Your Gran's not really there, you know," Mrs. Entwhistle said softly. "Her spirit isn't there, just a body she didn't need anymore."

"Oh, sure, like *you'd* know. Old people always think they know everything."

"I don't know everything, but I know that much. Is that why you're taking drugs, because you're grieving for your grandmother?"

But Mia didn't answer. She moved back into the shelves, sweeping her tiny penlight over the labels, singing, "The Candy Man can, 'cause he mixes it with love and makes the world taste good."

Mrs. Entwhistle suddenly felt swimmy-headed. Neither a shopping cart nor a cane could keep her upright when the store suddenly tipped sideways and dumped her on the floor. The girl heard her soft "oof!" as she landed.

"Hey! Old lady? Are you all right?" Mia peered through the grille and spotted Mrs. Entwhistle sitting on the floor, holding her head with both hands. "Hey, do you need help?"

When there was no answer, Mia rolled up the grille a couple of feet, scrambled over the counter on her belly and crawled over to Mrs. Entwhistle.

"Are you okay, ol' lady?"

"I think I am. Just got all over shivery for a minute and then I was on the floor. I fell and bumped my head earlier. That's why I got locked in tonight. I was unconscious when the store closed." She gingerly patted the back of her head.

"Let me see." Mia parted Mrs. Entwhistle's hair and peered at her skull. "Oh, wow. You have a big bump. You should probably see a doctor."

"Well, I'll put that on my To-Do list for when I get out of this store," Mrs. Entwhistle said tartly. "I obviously can't go out the way you came in."

"No, that won't work. Did you try phoning someone?"

Mrs. Entwhistle shot her a disgusted look. "Of course, I tried phoning. My phone's dead. Do you have one?"

"Nope. Can't afford a cell. Did you try the office?"

"Locked."

"Hmmm. Well, there's a security guy who sits in a little shack in the parking lot, but he's usually asleep. He's supposed to be monitoring the closed circuit cameras, so I usually put duct tape over the one in the pharmacy. In case he looks, all he'll see is a blank screen. I forgot to do it this time, though."

"Doesn't the pharmacist notice that pills are missing?"

"Nope, not so far, anyway. I just take a few out of random bottles. The thing is not to get greedy."

Mrs. Entwhistle thought that over. "I'd say you're not much of an addict if all you do is swallow a few pills a visit. It's more of a joy-ride for you, isn't it?"

Mia grinned. "It gives me something to do at night."

"But at your age! Seems like my kids were always out with friends at night when they were your age. Don't you have friends?"

Mia looked away. "No," she said shortly.

Mrs. Entwhistle nodded. "Okay, then. Your business. My business is getting out of here. How about if I deliberately set off the alarm? I'm surprised I haven't, already. When the police come, I'll explain what happened."

"Give me time to get back up on the roof and away from here," Mia said.

They turned back to the pharmacy. On Mia's midnight forays, she'd never ventured into the store itself. She hadn't thought to secure the heavy metal grill in the pharmacy when she raised it to help Mrs. Entwhistle, and it had gradually rolled back down to rest on the counter. When she gave it a push, there was a click as the lock engaged. The vent cover that led to her escape route still hung open, and the mess she'd made of the pill bottles was clearly visible. It wouldn't take a master detective to figure out what was what.

"Oh, boy. I'm in for it now," Mia sighed. "Anybody with half an eye can see what I've been up to, and

I'm trapped in here just like you are."

"You only got trapped because you tried to help me. I feel bad... but you *were* robbing the pharmacy, after all. There are always consequences for the choices we make," Mrs. Entwhistle said virtuously. "If I hadn't chosen to visit the store at the last minute, I wouldn't be here, either."

Mrs. Entwhistle and Mia gazed at each other in mutual consternation; then Mrs. Entwhistle felt a familiar rumbling in the vicinity of her stomach. She knew the message well: You Must Eat. Now. It was low blood sugar, she always explained, when her need for food suddenly became an embarrassing priority.

"It's been a long time since supper, and it will be a long time until breakfast," she explained to Mia. "I need to eat, or I'll get cranky."

"Okay," Mia said agreeably. "Let's go see what they've got in the deli, then. Might as well, since we've got nothing else to do." She led the way.

The deli proved to be a treasure trove. The cold shelves were full of enormous vats of prepared food. Mrs. Entwhistle felt bad about dipping into two-pound containers to get just a spoonful, but she said, "Needs must when the devil drives."

To which Mia said, "Huh?" and Mrs. Entwhistle replied, "Never mind."

They helped themselves to pasta salad, ham sandwiches, and fruit, then cruised the bakery aisle for dessert. After a debate between the merits of pecan pie and chocolate cake, they compromised by having a piece of each.

"Now if I could just have a cup of tea," Mrs. Entwhistle sighed, patting her lean midriff.

"No problem." Mia grabbed a quart of iced tea from the cooler, found a cup, filled it and popped it into the microwave. She really had a most remarkable economy of movement, Mrs. Entwhistle reflected.

Restored by calories and caffeine and feeling almost like her old self, Mrs. Entwhistle felt she needed to walk off her meal. She pushed her shopping cart up and down the clothing aisles. The counters were loaded with heaps of sweaters, sweatshirts, pajamas, shirts, pants, underwear, shoes, and jackets.

"Oh, look, this is cute," Mia exclaimed, pulling up a tee-shirt printed with butterflies. "I'll try this one."

"You can't just take it," Mrs. Entwhistle said.

"What do you think we did with all that food?"

"Well, but I'm keeping track, and I plan to pay for

everything."

"I don't." Mia slipped the tee over her shirt.

"That's called stealing."

"Yeah. I'm a thief. Remember why I'm here?'"

Mrs. Entwhistle shrugged. Although glad for Mia's company in the big, echoing store, she couldn't take on the moral rehabilitation of this strange girl. Besides, she didn't believe in giving advice. No one ever took it, anyway.

Mrs. Entwhistle checked out a bin of cardigans and fingered one in soft pink. She was chilly. It felt just right when she tried it on.

"I believe I'll buy this one," she said.

"Some call it buying; some call it stealing."

"Now stop that. I intend to pay...."

Her protests were cut short by a loud "Hello? Anyone there?"

Quick as a flash, Mia ducked behind a counter and motioned for Mrs. Entwhistle to get down, too.

"Why should I?" Mrs. Entwhistle whispered, but she knelt. Mia seemed so furtive it was catching.

"It's that darn security guard," Mia whispered back. "Tonight of all nights he looks at the CCTV feed. He must have spotted us."

"Well, that doesn't make this *my* fault," Mrs. Entwhistle hissed. "After all, you're the one who broke in. I just got left in here by mistake."

Footsteps warned them of the guard's approach. They both fell silent and remained still.

"Hello? Is anybody there? You might as well come out; I saw you on the security camera."

Mrs. Entwhistle and Mia didn't stir.

"You're in big trouble, breaking and entering like this. It's a felony or something. I'll call the police. You'll go to jail."

Mia's fearful intake of breath galvanized Mrs. Entwhistle. Her motherly instincts kicked in, and she rose to her full height rapping her cane sharply.

"I'm right here," she said, stepping out from behind the counter and walking away from Mia like a mother bird who flies away to distract attention from her babies.

The security guard shone a very bright light in her face. "What the hell? You're an old lady!" he exclaimed.

"Well, thank you for informing me of that fact," Mrs. Entwhistle said, shading her eyes. "I hadn't noticed, but now that you've pointed it out, why, I believe you're right: I *am* an old lady. Kindly get that light out of my face."

The guard shifted the beam. "What are you doing in the store at night?"

"I slipped and fell in your restroom and got knocked out. When I came to, the store was closed."

"You slipped? And fell? And lost consciousness?"

"That is correct."

Apparently, "slip and fall" were weighty words in the retail world, because there was a new carefulness in the guard's manner.

"You'd better sit down," he said, taking Mrs. Entwhistle's arm and pulling her toward a chair. "I'll call for an ambulance."

"I've been sitting. In fact, I've had a nap. No need for an ambulance; I just want to get out of here and go home now. I'll come back tomorrow and pay for the items I've used. Here, I've kept track."

A sudden movement caught their eyes as Mia scuttled from one hiding place to another. *Drat the girl, why couldn't she have stayed put?*

The guard swept his flashlight into the corner where Mia cowered. "You! Come out of there!"

Mia rose and came forward slowly to stand beside Mrs. Entwhistle.

"You're the one I saw on the pharmacy camera," the guard said. "What's your name, and what are you doing in this store in the middle of the night? You slip and fall, too?"

Mia stared at the guard mutely.

"Now I *am* going to call the police. I nabbed me a burglary ring. I bet you two are working together. Pretty clever, having an old lady for a beard. Let's see what you got in your pockets."

Mia turned her empty pockets inside out and shrugged. Mrs. Entwhistle bristled.

"The contents of my pockets are none of your concern," she said. "*I'm* the injured party here, remember?"

"Yeah, sure you are, lady. Tell it to the judge." He pulled out his cell phone, but hesitated and stood thinking for a few seconds. "Unless...no harm done, right? You didn't get away with anything."

"This sweater," Mrs. Entwhistle said, "And we ate some food in the deli. I've got a parasol and a cane, too. I intend to pay for everything."

"Look, nothing has actually been taken out of the store, has it? So, technically, no crime."

Mia bit her lip and kept silent about the drugs circulating freely in her veins.

He continued. "You know, we could just forget all this ever happened. If you make it worth my while, I'll let you go on your way."

Mrs. Entwhistle looked puzzled, then indignant. "Worth your while? You mean bribe you? You should be ashamed of yourself! Don't you get a paycheck for doing your job?"

She felt the jab of Mia's sharp elbow in her ribs and remembered that while the chances of her ending up in a cell were miniscule given her age and obvious respectability, it was a certain destination for the girl. The guard looked down at his cell phone again, his finger poised.

"Wait a minute," Mrs. Entwhistle said. "Let me just think for a minute. My...niece, here, she came in with me, and, uh, she was in another part of the store when I fell. She came looking for me when I didn't show up, and she... she couldn't get me to wake up, and she was too worried to leave me. And then the store closed, and she was trapped in here with me."

Doris Reidy

"Why didn't you call for help? You got phones."

"My phone's dead, and my niece doesn't have her phone with her."

"First teenager in the history of the world, then," the guard said. "Okay, whatever. How much money you got on you?"

Mrs. Entwhistle pulled out her wallet, extracted all the bills and fanned them out. She'd just been to the bank, so she had more money than she usually carried. "Let's see: there's $148."

"Jeez. Hardly worth it."

"Take it or leave it; it's all I've got." Mrs. Entwhistle held out the money and he stepped forward and snatched it from her hand.

"Now then; get us out of here," Mrs. Entwhistle said. "A deal's a deal."

"You'll have to go out the service entrance around back. I can't open the front doors because the code has to be entered on the computer in the guard shack."

They followed the guard to the back of the store and down a flight of concrete stairs. He walked slower and slower. Finally, he stopped and turned to face them.

"I been thinking," he said. "If you decide to sue the store because you slipped and fell, then all this will come back on me. Or maybe you'll just rat me out to the manager. Either way, I'll get fired, and I need this job, crummy as it is. Maybe I'm doing the wrong thing here."

"You certainly *are* doing the wrong thing," Mrs. Entwhistle said. "I'm glad you see it. A young man like you, your whole life ahead of you—I hate for you make such a bad decision."

"Look, lady, you don't know me; you don't know anything about me. My life isn't still ahead of me; it's all but over. I got troubles, big troubles." He plopped down on a step and put his head in his hands.

Mrs. Entwhistle and Mia exchanged glances. What next? Would this strange night never end? Since she seemed to be the only functioning adult present, it was up to her to make some sense of all this. She sat down, too.

"What's your name?" she asked.

"Jerald."

"Do your friends call you Jerry?"

"They might, if I had any friends. No, it's Jerald, always has been plain old Jerald. Sometimes I think my whole life might have been different if I'd had a nickname, been one of the gang, like."

Mrs. Entwhistle ignored his whiney tone. "Well, then, Jerald, what seems to be the trouble?"

"Everything! My life sucks. I blew off college and flunked out. Then I married too young and had too many kids. I have to do any kind of work I can get, and believe it or not, this crappy job is a step up for me. I work days at McDonald's, and then I'm so tired I fall asleep in the guard shack at night, so I'll probably lose this job when my boss figures it out. My wife yells at me because we've got overdue bills, and the babies scream night and day. Even my dog bit me. And now I've got you two to contend with."

Mrs. Entwhistle didn't speak. Mia backed up a couple of steps and sat down quietly.

Jerald continued in a strangled voice. "I can buy groceries for the week with your money, but if you turn me in, I'll lose this job and have to find another. I'm only twenty-four, but I feel like I'm a hundred." He gulped, and Mrs. Entwhistle realized he was actually crying.

She reached over and patted his shoulder. "There, there, Jerald. Nothing is ever as bad as it seems at night when we're tired. I'm sure you're doing the best you can. You need a little help right now and that's nothing to be ashamed of. Let's think what your options are."

"I don't have any," Jerald wailed. "I'm trapped like a rat, and it's my own damn fault."

"One thing I know for sure is that self-pity will sink you," Mrs. Entwhistle said firmly. "And another thing I know is there are always options. We may not like 'em, but there's always a way to work around things. Now let's try again. Have you asked your parents or your wife's parents for help?"

"My folks say I've flung every opportunity they've given me back in their faces, and now I'm on my own. Nina's mother is a widow living on Social Security. Even a creep like me can't take her money."

"I see. Could Nina get a job?"

"We've got three kids under four. The cost of day-care would be more than she could earn."

"Have you considered learning a trade so you don't have to depend on minimum wage jobs?"

"Takes time and money. I got neither." Jerald took a big, shuddering breath. "Sometimes, I think I'll just leave. You know, just get on a bus."

"Why don't you go, then?"

"The kids, I guess. I love 'em, in spite of the screaming." Jerald smiled ruefully.

"What about Nina? Do you love her, too?"

"I did. We were crazy in love. Now…I don't know. We don't talk about anything except bills and kids. We can't afford to do anything fun. I'm hardly ever home, and when I am, I'm exhausted. She's stuck with the kids day and night; it's a tough life for her, too."

Mrs. Entwhistle said nothing. She breathed in and out evenly. Presently, Jerald's breathing matched hers. She sensed the tension in his body relax a bit.

"If money were no object, what would you like to do?" she asked quietly.

"What I really love is to work outdoors. When I had time, before all the kids came along, our yard was the prettiest one on the block, and we had a big vegetable garden. It's gotten out of hand now, just like everything else in my stupid, sucky life."

"Self-pity, Jerald. Avoid it like poison-ivy."

"Yeah, whatever. But there's no money in that kind of work, not enough to support a family."

"Yet it seems I see a landscaper's truck every time I turn around," Mrs. Entwhistle observed.

"I don't want to just mow yards and edge driveways. I want to be a real gardener, planting and harvesting and growing things people would eat."

"And what stands in your way?"

"Jeez, you don't have much grasp of the real world, do you?" Jerald sounded angry. "I got three kids, remember? And a wife who don't work. And two crummy jobs that barely put food on the table and pay the rent. When do you think I'd have time to start my own gardening business?"

"It does seem insurmountable, doesn't it? I guess it's just one of those hopeless dreams that you'll never realize," Mrs. Entwhistle said, her tone philosophical. "Oh, well, plenty of people go through life unable to do what they really want. I guess you'll get by."

"Well, if I could just find someone to take a chance on me, give me a hand up, you know, I really think I could do it."

"Oh, that would be impossible. Where would you ever find anybody like that?"

"I'd like to work on a farm that sells produce and flowers directly to restaurants. Then I could learn as I worked, and maybe get to take home some of the produce that they'd be throwing out. Not slop, just vegetables that don't look as pretty. Nina's a really good cook. She can make all kinds of vegetarian dishes. She'd like to be a caterer when the kids get bigger, or maybe a personal chef."

Mrs. Entwhistle said, "Hmmm."

"I know this guy, he's a waiter at one of the farm-to-table restaurants in town, and he said he could maybe introduce me to the farmer that supplies their produce. I'd offer to do anything just to learn the business. 'Course, I'd have to have enough money saved to tide me over until I got going good, and I can't save a dang dime. It takes all I earn just to live."

Mrs. Entwhistle pursed her lips and nodded.

"Unless—maybe Dad might stake me if I could show him a good business plan, convince him and Mom that I'm really serious about it."

"Parents tend to be forgiving when they see a real effort," Mrs. Entwhistle said.

Behind them, Mia cleared her throat. Jerald scrubbed a hand over his face and got to his feet. He held out a hand to help Mrs. Entwhistle up, too. He reached into his pocket, pulled out her money and handed them to her. "Sorry about that. I wasn't thinking right. Thanks for, well, for listening and giving me good advice."

"I didn't give you any advice at all, Jerald. You figured it out for yourself."

Mrs. Entwhistle smiled, and Jerald smiled back.

"So I guess I'd better get you two out of here before the early re-stocking starts."

Mia shook her head. "Wait a minute, Jerry. I got into the store through the roof, and you spotted me in the pharmacy. There's a mess in there I didn't have time to clean up. It'll all be on the security camera footage. I don't want you to get fired because of me. Not now, when you've got a dream."

"I appreciate that. But why'd you do it? I mean, you're a pretty, young girl, you must have better things to do. So why go to so much trouble to break into the Bargain Barn?"

She hung her head. "Sometimes life gets...bad, you know? I do crazy things so I don't have to feel it for a little while. If you'd just unlock the grille and let me back into the pharmacy, I'll put everything where it belongs and go out the way I came in. Maybe you can delete the CCTV tape? If that's not asking too much?"

For a minute, Jerald looked like the father he was. He all but shook his finger at Mia. "You shouldn't break into places. You'll get caught, and the next guy won't be as understanding as I am. You don't want to go to jail, a girl like you. It'd be on your record forever."

"Yeah, I get it. It's stupid, I know that. Just help me not go to jail tonight, okay?"

"You have to promise you won't break into the Bargain Barn ever again," Jerald said sternly.

"Jerry, I not only promise that, but if you help me, I'll come around and give Nina a hand with the kids. I like kids. I wouldn't want to be paid or anything. Just a favor for a favor."

Mrs. Entwhistle held her breath while Jerald thought it over. These two young people were balanced on the edge of something. The wrong word from her could ruin it.

"C'mon, then," Jerald said, and led the way back into the store to the pharmacy.

He unlocked the grille and rolled it up a couple of feet. Mia skinned over the counter on her belly.

"You sure you can get back out?" he asked, eying the dangling grate cover dubiously.

"Done it before," Mia said, whisking the pill bottles back into tidy lines and blowing the pill dust away. "Sorry, but I didn't know you then. Won't happen again."

She stepped to the counter beneath the grate and hopped up. Pausing, she looked back at Mrs. Entwhistle. "Thanks, old—I mean, ma'am. We had some fun, didn't we? I hope your head is okay."

Mrs. Entwhistle smiled and nodded. Mia hoisted herself into the opening, and pulled the grate shut behind her. They heard her progress as she made her way through the air duct. Then she was gone.

They both heard movement and conversation at the same time. "Uh oh, it's the early stock crew," he said, looking wildly around for a place to conceal themselves. "We didn't get you out of here in time. Now I'm in for it."

"Jerald. Relax. Let me handle this. Just follow my lead," Mrs. Entwhistle said. She took Jerald's arm and led him in the direction of the restrooms. At the door of the ladies' room, she lowered herself carefully to floor and arranged her limbs in awkward positions. "Now kneel down beside me and act like you're taking my pulse," she whispered, replacing the whisper with a convincing groan just as a woman with a cart of supplies approached.

"What happened here?" the employee said. "Why is this lady on the floor? And why is she in the store when we're not open?"

"Well you may ask!" Jerald said, displaying a talent for acting he likely didn't know he had. "Go get the manager. We've got a problem."

The employee abandoned her cart and scurried away, casting an anxious glance back over her shoulder. Jerald helped Mrs. Entwhistle up and walked her to a chair in the snack bar.

"Very good, Jerald," she said softly. "I'll do the next bit."

The manager came running. "What's happened?" he asked. "Ma'am, are you all right? Have you been in the store all night?"

"Yes," Mrs. Entwhistle said, pressing a shaky hand to her brow. "I slipped on the wet floor in the ladies' room and when I woke up, the store was dark. My head, oh, my head!"

She showed him the large bump.

"This nice security guard found me, and I don't know what would have happened if he hadn't. I got a few items before I fell, they're right here in my cart, and I'll pay for everything."

"We wouldn't dream of letting you pay for anything. This is a most unfortunate occurrence, most unfortunate. The Bargain Barn is entirely at your service. I'll call for an ambulance."

"No, no, I don't need an ambulance. I just want to go home."

"Do you feel able to drive?"

"I drive a scooter, and no, I don't think I feel quite up to riding home on it just yet."

"Jerald, get a truck out of the garage, load up this lady's scooter and take her home. Ma'am, someone from our Risk Management Department will be in touch to make sure you're all right. If you'd just put your name and contact information on this form."

She did.

"Is there anything—anything at all—I can do for you, Mrs.," he glanced at her paperwork, "er, Arnthistle?"

"Well. Maybe just one little thing. I'm giving a shower today, and, thanks to being locked in your store overnight," Mrs. Entwhistle touched the back of her head and looked at the manager significantly, "I won't have time to make cheese straws. Do you suppose I could have a couple of boxes of yours from the bakery? They're almost as good as homemade. Oh, and the parasol. Don't forget the parasol. And this cane. And my sweater. And we, I mean, *I* ate some stuff."

The manager brushed away all her protests and offers to pay as he led her out of the store and helped her into the truck. She sampled a few cheese straws on the way home and passed the box to Jerald. Really, they weren't bad. The sun was just coming up as Jerald pulled into her driveway.

He paused before getting out to unload her scooter. "Mrs. Entwhistle, thank you for what you did tonight."

"Why, I didn't do anything but fall down, knock myself cuckoo and get locked in a store."

"Yeah, but that changed everything for me. Someday I'll bring you a basket of vegetables I grew myself. You just wait, I'll do it."

Mrs. Entwhistle said, "Jerry, I wouldn't miss it for the world."

Mrs. Entwhistle's Big Birthday

Turning eighty. Almost eighty. Pushing eighty. The Big Eight-Oh.

No matter how she phrased it, Mrs. Entwhistle couldn't get her mind around the birthday that was fast approaching. She'd have preferred to ignore it, but everyone she knew was determined to mark the occasion. What was it about other people's milestones that brought out an overwhelming urge to rub it in? Er, celebrate.

For weeks Diane and Tommy had been calling almost daily with ideas, each more far-fetched than the last. Mrs. Entwhistle appreciated their efforts, but she drew the line firmly at bagpipers.

Some prospects about her birthday were inviting, she had to admit. Dex and Lara were coming from Washington, D.C. for the weekend. She considered any time she spent with them to be a party, and especially now that Lara was expecting their first baby. Seeing Dex jittery with pride and concern was all Mrs. Entwhistle needed to put her in a good mood.

And Pete and Sheila Peters called to say they'd set up an appointment with a photographer for Mrs. Entwhistle and her namesake, baby Corrie. Mrs. Entwhistle hated the way she looked in photographs; surely, she was better looking than that! But she warmed to the idea of having pictures made with Corrie. The child would always know for whom she was named. It gave Mrs. Entwhistle a pleasant little thrill of immortality.

Even Booger had turned thoughtful, asking if she wanted a load of manure for her birthday.

"Them flower beds just soak it up," he'd said, eyeing the beds judiciously, thumbs hooked in the straps of his overalls. "I can't gift-wrap it, and it don't smell so good, but maybe you'd find it useful."

Everyone meant well, Mrs. Entwhistle knew, and she appreciated the affection that prompted them. But still, it was embarrassing. Maxine was the only one who understood. Her own eightieth birthday was only a couple of months after Mrs. Entwhistle's.

"You just have to let people have their way," Maxine advised. "I know you'd rather downplay it, but folks love you, and they want to show it."

"Well, I'm not against being loved," Mrs. Entwhistle replied. "But I feel silly, such a fuss being made over an old lady like me."

"Look at it this way: it's more for them than for you. It's important for them to be able to look back after you're gone and think, we really did the old dear proud."

They laughed and Maxine gave the front porch swing a gentle push with her foot. How many problems had been solved on that swing? How many cups of tea and bowls of homemade soup had been consumed there? How often had Mrs. Entwhistle curled up under an old quilt and let the night sounds comfort her when she couldn't sleep after Floyd passed?

Mrs. Entwhistle wondered what would happen to her old house after she was gone. Her will was drawn up, and each child had a copy, along with her banking information and computer passwords. A few precious things had been left directly to individuals. Maxine would get the quilt she and Mrs. Entwhistle had labored on for years. Diane and Tommy would get the quilts Mrs. Entwhistle's mother made. Neither of them would want the house; they had their own homes, their own families and memories. They'd sell the house and split the profits. Each would take a little something, maybe the gate leg table or the antique trunk, and offer a few mementos to her friends. The rest, her furniture and linens and clothing, would become junk the instant she passed. Nobody would want Floyd's old recliner with the duct tape holding the lever on. Nobody would want Mrs. Entwhistle's best and second-best pantsuits, or her ancient winter boots, or her bureau full of half-worn-out underwear and half-used-up grooming products. A big dumpster would be summoned and filled with the detritus of her life. She sighed. *Sic transit gloria mundi.* Thus passes worldly glory, such as her modest share of it was.

Her mind refused to accept the idea of a world without herself in it, so she stopped thinking about it. She was alive and kicking now, today, this minute, and that's what mattered. She planted her cane on the floor to stop the swing.

"I could eat," she said. "Want to go down to the Busy Bee Diner and get BLTs?"

~*~

Part of the great milestone birthday, and one that

her children especially insisted on, was that Mrs. Entwhistle should get a "good check-up." Obediently, she called to make an appointment with her doctor.

"What do you mean, Dr. Evers retired? I didn't hear a thing about it," she said to the receptionist. "I'm glad for him and all. Doctoring is hard work, being on his feet all the day long and putting his hands on sick folks. But still, I wish I'd have been told."

"Dr. Evers didn't want a fuss," the receptionist said. "He got a doctor to replace him so his patients would continue to receive care without a hitch."

"I can understand that," Mrs. Entwhistle murmured. "Sure can. So I guess I'll come see the new man, if you'll kindly give me a time."

"New *woman*," the receptionist said with a laugh. Mrs. Entwhistle could tell she delighted in springing this information on the unwary. "Her name is Dr. Natalie Dettler-Ross, and she's a real sweetheart. I know you'll like her."

After she hung up, Mrs. Entwhistle was ashamed of her initial feeling of dismay at the prospect of a young female physician. *I've never had a woman doctor before, but I know there are about as many women as men in medicine these days. I have to stop thinking like an old relic. Even if I am one.*

On the day of her appointment, she waited on the examining table in her skimpy paper gown. For lack of anything more interesting to do, she read a chart hanging on the door that listed heart attack symptoms. *Huh. Quite a list.* It sounded like a tall order for any physician to take care of all that. Not that she intended to have a heart attack, but if she did, she hoped this young lady was equal to the task.

It would have been more reassuring if Dr. Dettler-Ross, when she appeared, hadn't looked about twelve. Her blond hair hung straight down her back, her shoulders inside the white coat were narrow, and her pretty face was scrubbed as clean as a baby's. She thrust out a competent hand to shake Mrs. Entwhistle's.

"I'm Natalie Dettler-Ross," she said. "And you're Cora Entwhistle. I'm pleased to meet you. What brings you here today?"

"Pleased to meet you, too," Mrs. Entwhistle said. "My daughter insisted that I have a physical because I'm going to be eighty soon. I feel fine, hardly ever have a sick day, but you know kids. Or maybe you don't, yet."

Dr. Dettler-Ross laughed. "I'm older than I look," she

said. "I've got three kids. I think your daughter is right to encourage you to get some base-lines laid down while you're in good health. Let's have a look at you."

Mrs. Entwhistle endured the indignities of an exam and decided it was restful to know that the person examining her wrinkled old body was a fellow-female. She took deep breaths, said "ah," stuck out her tongue, squeezed the doctor's hands, looked to the left and to the right. She demonstrated that she could rise from a chair with no hands, bend and straighten, raise her arms over her head and step up on a foot-high riser.

"Did you dress yourself and drive yourself here today?" Dr. Dettler-Ross asked.

Mrs. Entwhistle blinked in surprise. "Who else would have done it?"

"Are you ever afraid or uncomfortable in your home?"

"I'm the only one there except for my dog, and I like his company. What kind of questions are these? Do I seem like I belong in the old folks' home?"

"Sorry, Medicare requirements, you know. How is your driving, by the way? Still feel confident behind the wheel? Any accidents?"

"I ride a scooter. Look out the window and you'll see it. That Vespa there. I just ride around town, not at night, but I don't have much call to go out at night, anyway."

"Well, Mrs. Entwhistle, everything looks good. I'd like to do an EKG today, just to make sure your heart is as normal as it sounds through the stethoscope. And I want you to stop by the lab on your way out and leave some samples. I don't expect to see anything worrying, but it's routine. You'd be healthy and vigorous for a fifty-year-old, let alone someone who is looking at her eightieth birthday. Congratulations."

Feeling as if she'd earned it, Mrs. Entwhistle stopped at the Dairy Queen on the way home and got a Blizzard.

~*~

Approaching her house, she saw the sun glinting off something on the front porch—something that hadn't been there when she left home. Squinting, she discerned that she was looking at a bouquet of Mylar balloons tied to one of the posts. HAPPY BIRTHDAY! they shouted. OVER THE HILL! MANY HAPPY RETURNS!

"My stars," she said.

She dismounted and leaned the scooter into the porch railing behind the hollyhocks. An enormous florist's arrangement stood at her door. She slipped the tiny card out of the envelope and read, "Happy Birthday! All our love, Dex and Lara." Tears swam in her eyes for a moment. Those sweet kids. She hated that they'd spent the money, especially on the balloons. But how were they to know she hated them? She'd never say so, and anyway, she loved the flowers. She decided to leave the balloons right where they were. They wouldn't be as annoying outside, and they'd make great decorations for the party.

The party. She'd struggled with the idea. Diane and Tommy wanted to rent the community room at the town hall and invite everyone, but Mrs. Entwhistle was horrified at the thought of all those gifts. Sure, they could say "no gifts." They could say it all day long, but in this small town people brought gifts to a birthday party.

"I don't want such a big fuss," she'd insisted over and over, until finally they had to believe her.

"Well, then, Mama, what do you want?" Diane asked.

"Could we just have a few people come by the house on Sunday afternoon? You know, like an open house. Folks who wanted to could just stop by after church, there'd be refreshments, and we could visit and all. We won't say it's a birthday party. Wouldn't that be okay?"

"If that's what you want, then that's what we'll do," Tommy said, exchanging a shrug with his sister.

It had all seemed simple enough, but the devil was in the details. Food, first of all. Mrs. Entwhistle had vetoed the children's plans to have the party catered by the Busy Bee Diner.

"Too expensive!" she'd cried. "I have plenty of time. I'll do some baking, make a few sandwiches, and brew iced tea. That will be plenty."

"Mama! You shouldn't have to cater your own party," Diane said.

"Tell you what, then. We'll say it's desserts only. You can supply a birthday cake, and I'll just whip up some cookies. How's that?"

"Well. Okay, I guess. If you insist on baking at all."

"It's no trouble. I like to bake."

That wasn't strictly the truth, but Mrs. Entwhistle knew Maxine, who did like to bake, would take over most of it.

With the venue and food settled, Mrs. Entwhistle

turned her attention to her house and yard. She wanted both to look their best for company. This summer for the first time in her life she'd hired a landscaping crew to do the mowing and edging. She still felt guilty about not doing it all herself, but she had to face the fact that it had gotten to be too much for her, especially in hot, muggy weather.

So the basics were in good shape. But the vegetable garden needed weeding, and she wouldn't feel right unless the house had a good going-over. She decided to talk to her neighbor, Ronnie Sue.

"Why, of course," that young lady said. "I'll help you clean. You keep your house so nice it won't need much, but we'll tweak it a little. And Biff will weed the garden."

"Does he know the difference between plants and weeds?" Mrs. Entwhistle asked. She'd had experience with Biff's work before. He was willing, but he suffered from not having been taught much in his growing-up years. Mrs. Entwhistle had her opinions about parents who were so preoccupied with their extra-marital love lives that they neglected their child's upbringing, but she didn't voice them; it wasn't Biff's fault. Still, she didn't want him pulling up her mint.

"You can show him which are plants and which are

weeds. I promise, he'll be real careful," Ronnie Sue said. "You know we'd do anything for you after the way you've helped us."

Mrs. Entwhistle had spent a portion of her Publisher's Clearing House winnings sending Ronnie Sue and Biff to hairdressing and plumbing schools, respectively. Now both were licensed in their trades and holding down good jobs. They'd married quietly a few months after Ronnie Sue's mother passed away, relieving the girl of her mama's care. Ronnie Sue and Biff had turned out well. Mrs. Entwhistle was too modest to claim any of the credit, but it did her good to know the young couple had taken advantage of the opportunities she'd been able to provide.

So the only thing left to do was get the word out. Mrs. Entwhistle decided to put a notice in the "Palaver," the gossip column in the daily newspaper. Editing the "Palaver" had been one of her duties when she'd been the oldest beat reporter in history. It had shaken her faith in human nature when she'd had to sift through the submissions and cobble them together in a column. The profanity, thinly-veiled threats and spiteful revelations had grieved her, but in spite of all that—or maybe because of it—the "Palaver" was the most widely-read feature in the newspaper. It ran on Fridays, and Herve' at the Busy

Bee Diner had learned to have extra sausage biscuits on hand for the crowd that gathered, spread newspapers on the tables and read aloud to each other.

She called her former editor, Jimmy Jack McNamara.

"Jimmy Jack, I want to put something in the paper," she said without preamble. "I want to put a line in the "Palaver" letting everyone know they're welcome to drop in at my house on Sunday afternoon for a neighborly get-together. Can you do that for me, please?"

Jimmy Jack agreed he could and would. He didn't mention he meant to do much more than that. He had great affection for his former community beat reporter. She'd saved him more than once from his natural inclinations toward indolence, ignorance and indecision. He ran Mrs. Entwhistle's invitation in a box at the bottom of the front page, along with a little editorial about how one of the town's leading citizens had cause for celebration. Everyone knew it was her birthday, anyway. When Mrs. Entwhistle saw it, she sighed and went straight to the kitchen to start another batch of cookies. There'd be a lot of people to feed.

Sunday she awoke to the patter of rain on the roof. Mrs. Entwhistle's groan caused Roger to lift his head and blink sleepily.

"Not rain, not today, Roger! There's no telling how many people will show up after Jimmy Jack made such a big deal in the paper. Where am I going to put them? I was counting on us being outside."

She levered herself out of bed and got into her robe and slippers. Tea. Tea would make everything better. Waiting for the water to boil, she stood at the kitchen sink and looked through the rain-speckled window at the battered petunia bed.

Lordy mercy.

Mrs. Entwhistle took stock. The porch could probably hold twenty people in a pinch. They'd need to be good friends, though; it would be tight. Others would have to come indoors. Counting the chairs in her living room, dining room and kitchen, she found she could seat another twenty. If it got too uncomfortable, people would just have to leave. Turning eighty was sure a lot of trouble.

"Yoo-hoo!"

Had to be Maxine. Only people their age called *yoo-hoo.*

"In the kitchen, Max."

Maxine's arms were full of baked goods. Mrs.

Entwhistle jumped up to relieve her of some of her load.

"More cookies, and I baked a couple more pound cakes. I figured we'd need 'em after Jimmy Jack ran that big notice on the front page."

"Oh, Max, what am I going to do with all those wet people?"

"It's going to clear up, honey. By noon, the sun will be shining and everything will dry off. When your guests arrive, it will be a perfect day."

"Huh. From your lips to God's ears," Mrs. Entwhistle said morosely. "Looks like an all-dayer to me."

"Now don't be negative, Cora," Maxine said. "The young count on us old folks to be cheery and positive." She winked.

Mrs. Entwhistle laughed. Maxine always could make her feel better.

"Did I tell you how I'm going to celebrate my eightieth?" Maxine asked. Mrs. Entwhistle shook her head. "I'm going to visit Geraldine."

"In Australia?"

"Yep. She's buying the plane ticket as a present. I'm going to stay for a whole month this time."

"Well, swanee, wasn't that sweet of Geraldine! She's always been a credit to her raising. It's pretty sneaky of you, though, to get out of having a birthday party of your own."

Maxine smiled. "That's why I'm going to enjoy yours so much."

Maxine was right about the weather. The skies cleared, and the sun came out by ten. As the day heated up, steam rose from the lavishly fertilized flower beds. Mrs. Entwhistle's hairdo went flat in the humidity, but she didn't have time to worry about it. She and Maxine kept right on working.

The dining room table looked beautiful, and Mrs. Entwhistle paused to admire it. The thick white tablecloth, starched and ironed to perfection, was anchored by Dex and Lara's flowers. Diane's birthday cake presided in the place of honor on the buffet. Mrs. Entwhistle had managed to prevail about candles. Eighty candles will burn the place down, she'd argued, and the volunteers at the fire department deserve to have Sundays off. Diane had finally agreed to one big candle.

Hearing a scratch at the back door, Mrs. Entwhistle hurried to let Roger in. He'd been allowed to make a solo trip to the back yard to relieve himself. Usually, she accompanied him to protect him from the next-door tomcat, and to make sure he actually remembered to do his business. He tended to be forgetful these days. Now he was preceded by a strong and unmistakable odor.

Roger had explored the flower bed. Roger had rolled in the manure.

Roger reeked.

"Oh, no, Roger! Today of all days! I don't have time to bathe you. You'll just have to be shut up in the bedroom until the party's over."

But Roger didn't think so. He barked and pawed at the door until it rattled. A couple of times he howled. Then he yelped like he'd just been run over by a truck. Mrs. Entwhistle couldn't stand it.

"The bathroom is spotless, and I don't want to wash a smelly little dog in there right before everyone arrives. What am I going to do?" she asked Maxine.

Maxine was sifting confectioner's sugar over a pound cake. She shook her head, tongue between her teeth as she concentrated on the cake. They heard a car door slam. It seemed the party was about to get started.

Mrs. Entwhistle's heart leaped. She remembered the symptoms on the chart in her doctor's office and decided she had them all. Probably she should call an ambulance and go straight to the hospital, but instead she pasted a frighteningly false smile on her face and went to the door.

"Booger! Thank goodness it's only you, I mean, it's you. Can you help me with Roger? He rolled in the manure."

"'Course I can. Where's he at?"

"Upstairs in my bedroom. First door, top of the stairs."

"Well, no, ma'am, I couldn't go into your bedroom." Booger looked down modestly.

"Oh, for heaven's sake! Just a minute, then."

Mrs. Entwhistle fetched Roger and held him at arm's length as she presented him to Booger.

"I'll go out back to the hose," Booger said. "You got any Fels Naptha? No? Well, dish soap'll do."

Mrs. Entwhistle closed her ears and heart to Roger's pitiful recital of all the things he hated about his bath. More guests were arriving. She stood on the front porch greeting them, forgetting she was still wearing her apron, the one that said, "Kiss the Cook." She wondered what had gotten into her normally undemonstrative neighbors and why there was so much giggling. There was a merciful absence of presents. She was surprised, but thankful. The last thing people her age needed was more stuff.

People wandered through the yard, admiring her flower beds. The sun shone benevolently on ladies in summer pastels and gentlemen in seersucker suits. There was a pleasant hum of conversation. Maybe this party was going to work out okay after all. Mrs. Entwhistle relaxed for the first time that day.

Too soon.

Yelping, Roger raced around the corner of the house at surprising speed for such an old dog. He was wild-eyed, soaking wet and sudsy as he tore through the sandals and pristine pant-legs of the guests, a trail of shrieks following him.

In pursuit came Booger. His sopping shirt flapped behind him and his large, lace-up, leather brogans were slick with soap. He careened after the bobbing, weaving dog, arms flailing. Inevitably, Booger lost his balance. Mrs. Entwhistle watched in horror as he skidded on the damp grass, scattering guests like bowling pins. Cookies and iced tea flew up to the heavens, then rained down on vulnerable heads. The air was filled with Booger's imprecations, in chorus with some of the guests'. Mrs. Entwhistle wouldn't have believed those church ladies even knew such words.

Her party was disintegrating before her eyes. Clearly, she had to do something and fast.

"Booger!' she roared. "Get up and stop chasing that dog. Roger, come here."

Roger did so, clearly preferring the devil he knew. Mrs. Entwhistle snatched him up and bore him inside to the laundry room. Grabbing a clean towel from the stack on the dryer, she dried him, soap suds and all.

"I'll give you a proper bath when this party's over, you poor old thing," she said quietly. Roger stopped struggling and looked up at her trustingly. "You need a nice nap, don't you, boy? Let's make you a little nest right here, out of the way."

When Mrs. Entwhistle returned to the front porch, the guests had already shaken off their misfortune along with the cookie crumbs. There was a buzz of talk and laughter about the runaway dog and his dogged pursuer. The story would become part of town folk-lore and live on in reminiscence. "Remember that time at old lady Entwhistle's birthday party?"

Booger stood abashedly in the corner, a steady plop-plop of water dripping in a circle around him. Mrs.

Entwhistle motioned for him to follow her, which he did, head down. He balked at the stairs, but she narrowed her eyes and fixed him with a steely gaze. He followed her up to her bedroom.

"Here," she said, opening the closet door. It wasn't a very big closet. Houses the age of hers didn't run to big closets, and she didn't have that many clothes anyway. A few of Floyd's shirts still hung on one side. She selected one and tossed it to Booger.

"Go into the bathroom, dry off, and put this one," she said.

"Cora, I couldn't...."

"Don't be silly. Floyd hasn't needed that shirt in a long time. It might be a bit small on you, but it'll be dry, at least."

She returned to her party. Dex and Lara had just arrived and were hugging their way through the crowd. Lara bore her very pregnant belly before her like the prow of a ship. Dex kept a wary eye on her at all times, as if she might explode. Actually, she looked like she could. Mrs. Entwhistle remembered those days of late pregnancy, the discomfort and anticipation tinged with dread at what was coming. She decided she wouldn't have missed it for anything, but she wouldn't do it again for a million dollars.

And then.

In her peripheral vision, she saw Floyd! That shirt, she'd know it anywhere— she'd ironed it dozens of times. She felt swimmy-headed. Closing her eyes against the encroaching blackness, she groped for the porch railing and hung on. Her whole life seemed to be unreeling in her mind. Could this be death? She'd read somewhere that when a person dies, her life flashes before her eyes. Talk about a party-pooper! She would become a town legend if she turned up her toes here and now. But the pictures in her mind's eye were so vivid that she stopped worrying and just... looked.

There were Tommy and Diane with strawberry-stained mouths after helping their daddy in the garden. She saw her wedding day, the faces of her family and friends turning to her like sunflowers as she walked up the aisle. Her high school graduation photograph, black-draped shoulders and hard-sprayed helmet hairdo. Tommy's birth, the abrupt release from pain, the amazing first glimpse of a human being she'd made. Maxine, maybe nine years old, skipping rope in the schoolyard, chanting:

Cora and Floyd
Sitting in a tree,

K-I-S-S-I-N-G
First comes love,
Then comes marriage
Then comes Cora
With a baby carriage.

Well, that part had come true. Her private film sped faster, retelling the story of her life. There were sad parts and times of frustration and fear. Mostly, it was good, though. Had she appreciated it while it was happening? She knew that sometimes she had, sometimes she hadn't. But she appreciated it now, like Jimmy Stewart in that Christmas movie. What a privilege it was to live to be old. It was well worth the price paid in regrets, losses, aches and pains.

She gave herself a good mental shake and grabbed at reality. For heaven's sake! It was only Booger in Floyd's shirt, that's all; not a visit from the dead and not a near-death experience.

Get a grip, Cora Entwhistle. Don't make a spectacle of yourself in front of all these people.

The swimmy feeling receded, and she opened her eyes just in time to be enveloped in one of Dex's comforting hugs.

"All right, Mrs. E.?" he asked in her ear.

"Of course, I am, honey," she said, feeling an irrepressible smile spread over her face. That smile always showed up when Dex did.

Mrs. Entwhistle scanned the gathering, realizing she hadn't seen Diane or Tommy since Diane delivered the cake earlier that morning. The grandchildren were all present and on their best behavior, running errands, passing out cookies and refreshing peoples' drinks like helpful little angels, but their parents were notably absent. Where could they be? One of them might be late, but surely not both, not for her birthday party. She noticed everyone checking their watches. Was her party that boring? Were people plotting a mass exodus at the earliest possible moment?

She heard a sound—put-put-put—that made her think of her scooter, and by the way, where *was* her scooter? She'd meant to put it in the garage instead of leaving it in the usual place against the porch railing. In all the excitement, she'd not noticed it wasn't there. In fact, she'd been so busy she couldn't remember when she'd last seen it.

Shading her eyes, Mrs. Entwhistle beheld her very own Vespa turn into the driveway, which she now realized had been left miraculously clear. Well, she guessed it was her scooter; it looked strangely lop-sided. Tommy was driving, and was that Diane sitting beside him? And sitting in what?

"What in the world?" Mrs. Entwhistle murmured.

Wearing huge grins, Tommy and Diane extricated themselves from the scooter, raising their clasped hands like prize-fighters. Amid cheers, Jimmy Jack climbed up on the top porch step. He pulled Mrs. Entwhistle to his side.

"Mrs. Entwhistle, I know you said no gifts, but, well, we're not a very obedient bunch. We like to see you tooling around town on your scooter, and we thought you needed your best pal beside you. We all went in together with your children, Diane and Tommy, and got you a sidecar. Now you can take Maxine with you, and even Roger."

Jimmy Jack produced a gift-wrapped package and handed it to Mrs. Entwhistle. Speechlessly, she opened it to find, nestled on a bed of tissue paper, two sets of pink goggles. The larger pair were labeled 'Maxine'; the smaller pair was Roger's.

"Oh, my goodness." Mrs. Entwhistle had to stop and collect herself. "I'm not often at a loss for words, but I just don't know what to say." She swallowed hard. "Y'all are too generous. I appreciate it with all my heart, but this is far too generous. I can't let you spend your money on me this way."

Jimmy Jack cut her off. "We knew you'd say that, so

we fixed it so you don't have a choice. It's a done deal; that sidecar is welded on. You and Maxine can ride off into the sunset. That is," he paused and cocked an eyebrow, "if you think you can handle it."

Mrs. Entwhistle's chin came up and her spine straightened. "Why, I don't see why I wouldn't be able to *handle* it," she said.

"Here." Tommy passed her the keys. "Try it out, Mama. Aunt Maxine, come on, honey. Hop in and take a ride with Mama."

He escorted the ladies to the scooter, one on each arm, and steadied Maxine as she stepped into the sidecar. When they were securely settled, Mrs. Entwhistle revved the scooter's motor. It responded, not with an ill-bred roar, but with a polite purr— much more suitable for their time of life. Cautiously, she backed out of the driveway and into the street. The scooter felt different with its new attachment. She puttered along, getting the feel of it. Then she put her foot down and they were off. They were only going thirty miles per hour, but it felt fast. Maxine let out a whoop, and Mrs. Entwhistle did, too.

"Whooee!" The wind snatched the word from her mouth and streamed it out like a banner.

Behind her was a sea of friends, waving and calling

encouragement. Beside her was her best friend, Maxine. Ahead... well, who knew? She might be old, her life might be winding down, but she had today, and really, that was all anybody had.

Today was enough.

End

ABOUT THE AUTHOR

Doris Reidy believes in second acts. Originally a non-fiction writer, she published articles in *Redbook, Writer's Digest* and *Atlanta Magazine*, among others, along with a monthly book review column for the *Atlanta Journal & Constitution.* After a long literary silence during which life intervened, she reinvented herself as a fiction writer at age 70. *Many Happy Returns, Mrs. Entwhistle i*s the fourth novel featuring formidable senior citizen, Cora Entwhistle.

Made in the USA
Columbia, SC
30 September 2023

23654639R00157